THE ROPER

Though this play is inspired by
actual historical events, it is a work of fiction.
All of the characters, events, and organizations
portrayed in this work are either products of the
author's imagination or used fictitiously.

The Roper

Copyright © 2014 by Will Dunne

ISBN-13: 978-1957328515

Published by Sordelet Ink
WWW.SORDELETINK.COM

THE ROPER

A PLAY BY
WILL DUNNE

The Roper was developed through table readings and stage readings at Chicago Dramatists, Russ Tutterow, Artistic Director.

The Roper had its world premiere on March 6, 2014, at The Den Theatre in Chicago, Illinois. The production was directed by Ron Wells, with scenic design by Andrew Hildner, lighting design by Cat Wilson, sound design by Mikey Moran, costume design by Rachel S. Parent, and props design by Vivian Knouse. The cast was as follows:

WILLIAM NEALY - John Luzar
LEWIS SWEGLES - Tony Bozzuto
PATRICK TYRRELL - Brad Woodard
TERRANCE MULLEN - Michael Downey
HERBERT NELSON/JOHN POWER - Robert Koon
JACK HUGHES - Ted Hoerl

Cast

William Nealy, *alias Billy Brown, a hack driver*

Lewis Swegles, *alias Jim Morrissey, ex-convict and informer for the U.S. Secret Service*

Captain Patrick Tyrrell, *Chief of the Chicago District of the U.S. Secret Service*

Terrence Mullen, *saloon owner and coney man*

Herbert Nelson,* *freight company operator and coney man*

Jack Hughes, *alias Shepherd, infamous Chicago coney man*

John Power,* *custodian of the Lincoln Monument*

*The roles of Nelson and Power
can be played by the same actor.

Time & Setting

Older Nealy's two monologues to the audience occur in August, 1896. Otherwise:

Act One spans a period of nearly three months, from late August to early November, 1876. Three scenes take place at a desk in the Chicago District Office of the United States Secret Service. The rest of the dramatic action takes place in the Hub, an Irish saloon in Chicago. Plain and dimly lit, the room has a long wooden bar with a mirror behind it. There are no stools since most customers drink standing up, and only a couple of old wooden tables with chairs. Other features include a billiards table, potbelly stove, glass tank on the bar with a live snake inside, and hollow plaster bust of Abraham Lincoln on a shelf over the mirror. There is a door and window to Madison Street outside and a door to the rear rooms where the owner lives and conducts private business.

Act Two begins on the evening of November 6, 1876, on a train platform. The rest of the actions occurs on Election Day, November 7, 1876. The setting is the tomb chamber of the Lincoln Monument at Oak Ridge Cemetery in Springfield, Illinois. Featuring marble walls and a tessellated black-and-white marble floor, the oval room houses the sarcophagus of Abraham Lincoln which is made of white marble and stands alone on trestles in the center. Etched into the end plate is a garland of oak leaves separating the name "LINCOLN" below from an inscription above: "With Malice Toward None. With Charity Toward All." Five numbered burial vaults line the rear wall, with the center vault open and empty. The tomb entrance is a steel door made of iron rods and usually padlocked. Visitors view the sarcophagus through this door. A few scenes take place outside of it. Most of the dramatic action occurs inside the tomb.

"A man's fame lasts longer than his life."

— *Old Irish proverb*

ACT I

Scene I

[The year is 1896. Older Nealy addresses us. He has a newspaper.]

OLDER NEALY

Once upon a time, a great and devouring fire swept through Chicago and burned it to the ground. This conflagration was so fierce, it felt like the gates of Hell had opened and the Devil himself was passing by. For years after, when the wind would blow a certain way, you could still smell it in the air: the smoke, the fire, the city that once was.

This is a story about a different kind of fire that sweeps through men's souls and changes who they are. I'm telling it to you now because of a promise I made on a train platform twenty years ago. Me name is William Nealy and you probably never heard of me. I'm only a hack driver from Waukegan, but I happened to know the man that this is about, and he told me what occurred. Even got me caught up in it meself, but only for a short time, thank God.

It's the summer of 1876, the Centennial. People is still talking about General Custer and the Seventh Cavalry being massacred at Little Big Horn a few weeks back. In the saloons, there's a new light-colored beer called Budweiser Lager. And across the nation, a fierce presidential race is now raging, with a Democrat named Tilden and a Republican named Hayes running neck and neck toward Election Day.

Election Day will be an important part of this story, but that's where it ends. Where it begins is three months earlier in the office of Captain Patrick D. Tyrrell, Chief of the Chicago District of the United States Secret Service.

SCENE II

[The U.S. Secret Service office in Chicago twenty years earlier in 1876. Captain Patrick Tyrrell is interviewing Lewis Swegles at his desk and taking notes. Swegles appears eager and anxious.]

TYRRELL

Have you ever been arrested?

SWEGLES

No, sir.

TYRRELL

Mr. Swegles, you are being considered for employment with the United States Secret Service. I suggest you be as forthright as possible. Have you ever been arrested?

SWEGLES

Yes, sir.

TYRRELL

Go on then. How many times and what for?

SWEGLES

Just once, sir. I was trying to sell some horses to a gentleman in Kenosha. Some confusion arose about the title of ownership. The gentleman did not take kindly to the confusion so he used his influence as a rich banker to have me arrested.

TYRRELL

Had you stolen the horses?

[Silence.]

Mr. Swegles?

SWEGLES

Yes, sir, I did steal them horses and that didn't make me look too good in the eyes of the jury, so I ended up for a short while in the Wisconsin State Penitentiary. *[Silence. Watches Tyrrell write.]* Do you have to write that part down?

TYRRELL

If you've been in prison, son, that's a fact I'm obliged to record.

SWEGLES

Then I hope you'll also write down that I have corrected the error of my ways. Which is why I am now seeking honest employment, such as a position with the Department.

TYRRELL

It's not really a "position" we're offering. As a roper, you would always use an alias and operate undercover. You would receive no credentials and you would never be allowed to represent yourself as a government agent – not even to avoid arrest or prison.

SWEGLES
  But I would still be getting the six dollars a day?

TYRRELL
  You would be getting five dollars a day. That's the standard
  rate.

SWEGLES
  Mr. Deane had said it would be six dollars a day.

TYRRELL
  Mr. Deane is one of Chicago's finest attorneys and a
  war hero who fought at Gettysburg, but he does not
  determine what ropers get paid. Is five dollars a day
  unacceptable?

SWEGLES
  Sir, it's more than twice what I ever earned for an honest
  day's work. And if you have doubts about hiring me due
  to my crooked background, I assure you that—

TYRRELL
  Young man, it is your crooked background that attracted
  me to you in the first place.

SWEGLES
  Huh?

TYRRELL
  Catching thieves is like catching fish. You have to use the
  right bait. Now, if you wanted to catch a thief and you
  baited his hook with a minister of the Gospel, you would
  be a fool because thieves and preachers do not naturally
  seek each other's society. In other words, it takes a thief
  to catch one. My concern about you, Mr. Swegles, is that
  your background is not quite crooked enough.

SWEGLES
  In that case, sir, you should know that I am far more

crooked than I look. Used to steal horses left and right, just never got caught at it, except for that time in Kenosha. I also been on different occasions a burglar, confidence man, pickpocket—

TYRRELL

It's counterfeiting I'm interested in. Mr. Dean led me to believe you had knowledge of the coney trade.

SWEGLES

Oh, yes, I do have such knowledge, sir, having associated with coney men while I was in prison. And may I add that, of all the crooks I met, the coney men was always the nicest.

TYRRELL

Do you think it's "nice" that coney men are destroying this nation's monetary system?

SWEGLES

No, sir, I don't think that's nice at all.

TYRRELL

It's what the sons of bitches are doing. After the war, half of all the paper money in this country was counterfeit. That's why the Secret Service was established.

SWEGLES

Sir, I didn't mean they was nice in the way a good person would be nice, but rather in the way a crook would be nice if you was to compare him to other crooks, such as, um, killers, for instance, who ain't usually nice at all.

TYRRELL

When ropers start out, they often underestimate the difficulty of using a false identity. Mr. Dean tells me, however, that you can present yourself well as an Irishman.

SWEGLES AS "MORRISSEY" [*With an Irish accent*]
From a glen near Brittas in County Wicklow, sir. But me poor mam and pap, they lost everything to the blight. So, they packed up the children – Gemma, Orla, Fiona, Claire, Dylan, Liam, Oisin, Shane, Colm, and me – and brung us to America to start life anew.

TYRRELL
How is it that a man with a German name speaks so well with an Irish tongue?

SWEGLES
Sir, I'm a fast learner and have an ability to remember things. I also have a friend from Ireland who talks a lot.

TYRRELL
Being a roper is dangerous work. Why would a young man such as yourself want to put himself in harm's way?

SWEGLES
I wish to do something for the good of society.

TYRRELL
And to what do we owe this noble ambition?

SWEGLES
Sir, I was walking down a road in Iowa one morning when I come upon a shed, an old shed with a corn fodder roof. Soon as I seen it, I knew there was a horse inside. A black beauty, too, as it turns out, what could fetch a high price. So, I decides to steal it. But as I go to nab that horse, I hear behind me a little voice: "Get out of my shed, you damned horse thief."

I turn and find a small girl in a white nightgown standing there with a big rifle pointed up at me. Now I'm looking down at that gun, but at her face, too. If you was to meet an angel from Heaven Above, this is the kind of face you would see.

"Now, darling," I says, "I ain't gonna steal your horse and I know you ain't gonna shoot me." Before I can say another word, she shoots me! Right here in the shoulder! I start running back to the road and she keeps cursing and shooting and cursing and—

TYRRELL
I hope no harm came to this girl.

SWEGLES
Only to myself, sir, and I still got part of the bullet in me to prove it. But once I got to safety, I had to ask, what would stir such hate in a child so sweet? That's when my eyes opened and I seen what I'd become: a damned horse thief with a bullet in his shoulder. So right then and there, in the middle of Iowa, I decided to be someone else. Someone good.

TYRRELL
Do you really believe people can change who they are?

SWEGLES
Sir, it's why I come to you wanting to be a roper.

[Tyrrell studies him curiously. Makes a final notation. Shows him a photograph.]

TYRRELL
This is the fish we're after, Jack Hughes, a notorious shover of counterfeit money and a disgrace to the Irish people. We have ample evidence to convict the bastard, but we don't know where he is. Your assignment is to find him. Do you understand?

SWEGLES
Yes, sir. Thank you, sir. Thank you very much.

TYRRELL
You will report to me daily, but we shall have no contact

outside this office. If we happen to see each other on the street, we shall pass by as if we were strangers. We do this for your protection. *[Hands him a piece of paper.]* Here is the address of an Irish saloon called The Hub. We believe that it may be a resort for counterfeiters. Get yourself known there as one of the boys. See what you can learn about Jack Hughes. Any questions?

SWEGELES

Yes, sir. I was just wondering, sir. When exactly, um, when do I get the five dollars?

Scene III

[The Hub the next day. A hot August afternoon. Mullen and Nelson play billiards in an otherwise empty saloon. Swegles as "Morrissey" enters from the street.]

SWEGLES AS "MORRISSEY"
  Good day to you, fellas! Now this here is the spot to be surely, quiet and cool!

[They ignore him. He looks around and approaches the bar where there is a live snake in a glass tank. As he leans down to inspect it, the snake suddenly strikes the glass. He leaps away.]

NELSON
  I believe the young man just met Bridgette.

MULLEN
  She's only a snake, mate, and she ain't poisonous, but she do bite. So, don't go sticking your hand in there unless what you need to partake of alcohol is a medical excuse.

MORRISSEY
  They call her Bridgette, do they? Seems like an odd name for a snake. Especially one what lives in a saloon. I guess now I seen everything eh?

MULLEN

Everything but the sign in the front window.

NELSON

Excuse me, Boss, but would you be referring to the large white sign in the front window that says "Closed?"

MULLEN

Aye, Nelson, that would be the very sign indeed what I was referring to. Must have escaped the paddy's gaze as he stumbled to the door in a state of thirst.

NELSON

Or perhaps, as he stumbled to the door in a state of thirst, he saw the large white sign in the front window that says "Closed," but, being an Irishman, didn't know how to read it.

MULLEN

Or maybe the paddy did read it, but decided to ignore it, thinking himself too high and mighty to have a large white sign what says "Closed" applying to the like of him.

MORRISSEY

All right, fellas, I do see the sign now and I'm sorry to disturb you, but could you at least tell me when the saloon will be open?

MULLEN

You got money in them pockets?

MORRISSEY

Yes, sir.

MULLEN

The saloon is open now.

MORRISSEY

That's more like it. I been traipsing around in that heat

all morning looking for work and I'm more than ready for a beer. The name is Morrissey. Jim Morrissey.

MULLEN
Beer is five cents. Let's see some cash on the bar.

MORRISSEY
[Puts out coin.] Here you go. And I'll tell you what, pour up three beers. One for each of us!

MULLEN
Nelson, you want another beer? I believe the paddy is buying.

NELSON
You sure his money is good?

MULLEN
You wouldn't be coming in here and trying to shove coney in me saloon, would you?

MORRISSEY
No, sir. Them is real nickels for real drinks.

NELSON
In that case, Boss, I'll take a whiskey. A "real" one.

MULLEN
The customer wants whiskey. Whiskey is fifteen cents.

MORRISSEY
[Puts out more coins.] That's no problem neither. I got the money right here. And like me uncle always says, a man in a saloon should have whatever it takes to make him happy.

MULLEN
Then I guess I'll be having a whiskey as well.

MORRISSEY
[Puts more coins on bar.] Make it three whiskeys. That'll be me celebration for getting out of Nebraska.

NELSON

What's wrong with Nebraska? I hear it's a dandy place to be.

MORRISSEY

Not if you're in prison for stealing horses. You fellas ever been in prison?

[Nelson and Mullen exchange a look.]

NELSON

I'm in the freight hauling business. They don't put you in prison for that.

MULLEN

That'll do about prison. Here's to good fortune for them what deserves it.

NELSON

And a little extra for our friend from Nebraska and his search for employment.

MULLEN

To that then, too. What the hell.

[They toast and drink.]

But he won't be finding no employment around here. Not even at the slaughterhouses.

NELSON

Don't listen to him. You can always get a good job at a slaughterhouse.

MULLEN

Not if you're Irish. Knock on any door in this town and they'll look at you like you got a disease no one wants to catch. And, even if you do find work, they'll pay you half what everyone else makes. From where in Ireland have you come?

MORRISSEY

From a glen near Brittas in County Wicklow, sir. But me poor mam and pap, they lost everything to the blight. So they packed up the children – Gemma, Orla, Fiona, Claire, Dylan, Liam, Oisin, Shane, Colm, and me – and brung us to America to start life anew.

MULLEN

[Eyes him coldly.] Wicklow, eh?

MORRISSEY

Yes, sir. Then a farm in Wisconsin. And then, when I was sixteen, I run off to sea.

MULLEN

I been beaten and robbed twice in me life. Both times it happened in Wicklow.

NELSON

We're not in Wicklow now, so let's have another round. This one's on me.

MULLEN

Them Wicklow people got the Devil inside 'em. Beaten bloody, I was, and robbed blind!

NELSON

This is what I call the "hour of aristocrats." Late enough in the day to have a drink but early enough to beat the crowd. I'm Herbert Nelson and that cheerful fellow is Terrance Mullen, but we usually just call him the Boss. Welcome to The Hub!

[Nelson and Morrissey drink. Mullen doesn't.]

MORRISSEY

Either of you fellas know a guy goes by the name of Jack Hughes?

[Nelson and Mullen exchange a look.]

MORRISSEY
While I was in prison, I met a coney man named Red.
And he says to me, "Morrissey, if you ever get back to
Chicago, be sure to go to a drinking saloon called The
Hub and ask for Jack Hughes. He's a first-class man what
can show you around to the right people."

NELSON
We don't know any Jack Hughes. Must be a different
saloon your friend told you about.

MORRISSEY
He wrote it for me here on this paper. See? "The Hub.
Two ninety-four west Madison."

[Mullen looks at the paper, crumples it, and tosses it aside.]

MULLEN
Come on, Nelson, we got a game to finish.

NELSON
Good luck to you, Jim Morrissey. You'll be needing it.

MULLEN
I've known a lot of men in me time what's been in prison.
He's the first one ever walked in the door bragging
about it.

[Back at the billiards table, Mullen takes his shot.]

Scene IV

[The Hub ten days later. A stormy day. Lightning and thunder. Shepherd, bearded, dozes at a table over his beer as Mullen works behind the bar. Morrissey enters.]

MORRISSEY

It's for glum days like this God gave us the gift of whiskey, so pour me a proper one, Boss. I'm in need of a little sunshine.

MULLEN

[Aside to Shepherd.] That's Morrissey. The one we was telling you about.

SHEPHERD

Pull up a chair, lad, and make yourself at home. They call me Shepherd is what they call me, but don't be getting the wrong idea now. I got nothing to do with sheep.

MORRISSEY

Please to meet you, Shepherd. Would you be a pal of Mullen there?

SHEPHERD
No one's a pal of Mullen, but I suppose I could pass for one if I had to.

MULLEN
Pay no mind to the like of him. I got plenty of pals and in high places, too.

[A cowbell rings from the rear. Mullen and Hughes look at each other anxiously.]

Be a good mate, Shepherd, and give a holler if any customers come in.

[Mullen exits to the rear with three drinks on a tray.]

MORRISSEY
What's going on in the back room?

SHEPHERD
They're having a meeting. In the saloon business, they have a lot of meetings.

MORRISSEY
You sure it's the saloon business they're talking about?

SHEPHERD
I guess what I been hearing is right. You are one curious lad.

MORRISSEY
Been looking for a man named Jack Hughes. That wouldn't be him back there, would it?

SHEPHERD
No, but I do know a fella named "John" Hughes. A railroad man like me.

MORRISSEY
The Hughes I'm after has certain associates what might help me get into a new line of work. And, just between us, Shepherd, it ain't the railroad business I got me eye on.

SHEPHERD

[*Looks him over.*] They say you got sent here by a fella named Red.

MORRISSEY

A coney man from Chicago. Went to Nebraska to shove five-dollar queer and ended up pressing it into the wrong hands.

SHEPHERD

So it's shoving the queer you'd be wanting to try?

MORRISSEY

I hear it's easy money if you have the right associates. Does that sound like the kind of associates your Mr. Hughes might have?

SHEPHERD

You could always ask him and see what he says.

MORRISSEY

So, you'll help me locate him?

SHEPHERD

Well, Morrissey, that depends on what it's worth to you. In a society run by banks, everything is worth something. You really a horse thief?

MORRISSEY

Used to be. Done some other thieving as well.

SHEPHERD

Now that's something makes me curious. Anybody can steal money. But a man what steals horses, he's got to be willing to wrestle with Nature, and that means he's got something unbridled inside him. It's the unbridled part what intrigues me.

MORRISSEY

I could say the same about some burglars I know. And

I've known a few in me time, I have, both in and out of prison. Billy Brown, Smiling Mike O'Connor. The most famous would be Frenchy the Burglar. Best thief this side of the Atlantic. Ever hear of him?

SHEPHERD
Frenchy the Burglar? Yes, of course, I have. D'you really meet him somewhere?

MORRISSEY
In prison last year, and we been fast friends ever since. Just got a letter from him last week. Wrote it to me from the Michigan City jail.

SHEPHERD
Wait a minute now. You got a letter written to yourself from Frenchy the Burglar?

MORRISSEY
Right here in me pocket!

SHEPHERD
Would it be possible for me to have a peek at that letter?

MORRISSEY
Well, Shepherd, that depends on what it's worth to you. In a society run by banks, everything is worth something.

[Nelson enters from the rear and addresses Shepherd.]

NELSON
Cornelius would like a word with you.

SHEPHERD
With me? What in hell would Cornelius want with the bleeding like of me?

[Nelson shrugs. Shepherd exits anxiously to the rear.]

NELSON

So, what do you think of our Jack Hughes? Is he what you expected?

MORRISSEY

Jack Hughes? Oh. No, sir, I – I didn't know he had grown a beard.

Scene V

TYRRELL

Congratulations, Mr. Swegles. In only ten days, you've accomplished what a team of officers has been unable to do for over a year. Thanks to you, Jack Hughes is off the street and we're one step closer to restoring confidence in our nation's money.

SWEGLES

Thank you, sir. It was but a stroke of luck, to be sure, but still I been wondering. Do I get my name in the newspaper for this?

TYRRELL

You're an undercover agent. All public thanks will go to myself and the officers who ran Hughes in.

SWEGLES

How will people know what I done?

TYRRELL

They won't. You were told how this works when you applied for the job.

SWEGLES

Yes, sir, but now that the job is over, I thought perhaps—

TYRRELL

Over? You said you wanted to work for the good of society.

SWEGLES

Yes, sir, and now that I done that, it would be nice to have proof of it.

TYRRELL

Proof of it for what?

SWEGLES

For my children, sir. I want them to know that their father, Lewis Cass Swegles, is a man to be proud of. A man who done something important.

TYRRELL

Bring them here then. I'll tell them what a fine roper you are. You have boys or girls?

SWEGLES

Neither yet, sir. I'm thinking ahead to the day I find me a wife and we start having children. First one. Then another. Lots of children. As we all gather 'round the dinner table, they'll be looking up at me and wanting to know—

TYRRELL

Sit down, Mr. Swegles.

SWEGLES

Huh?

TYRRELL

Sit. We'll worry about the children later.

[Swegles sits reluctantly.]

Terrance Mullen who runs The Hub. I'm told he's the type who could open fire on a man without an extraordinary amount of provocation. How does he strike you?

SWEGLES
He seems to fancy himself as a man of importance. But he's also a bit gloomy. Has a way of looking around as if something terrible is about to befall him.

TYRRELL
We suspect he's a fence for the same ring that employed Hughes, but Mullen knows how to keep his hands clean. We need to get the dirt on him. That's your next assignment.

SWEGLES
My, uh, next assignment?

TYRRELL
I want to know what goes on in that back room.

SWEGLES
Sir, this business of roping people in, it's more difficult than I expected.

TYRRELL
I understand, son. But, the more you do it, the more you'll learn to live with the danger.

SWEGLES
It ain't the danger. It's the pretending you're someone you ain't in order to gain a man's confidence. Even when you do it in the name of good, it has a way of eating you up.

TYRRELL
Son, I came to this country from Dublin when I was nine. Got an education and worked hard all my life, first in the police department, then in the Secret Service. Now I am

Chief of the Chicago District, a middle-class man with a family and a house in a respectable part of town. But when others in this country think of the Irish, it is not men like me they think of. No, it is men like Mullen and Hughes. Ignorant, lazy, untrustworthy micks. What I am attempting in my work here is not only to bring criminals to justice. It is to change how others in this country see the Irish. It is to show them that the Irish who come to America are to be welcomed and admired. I need a good roper to help me do that. This is noble work, Lewis. Work that will leave even your grandchildren in awe. Will you be a noble man and help me?

[He holds up a five-dollar bill. Swegles reaches out and takes it.]

Scene VI

[The Hub the next day. Late morning. No one is here. Morrissey enters. The rear door is ajar.]

MORRISSEY

  [Calls out.] Boss?

[No reply. He sneaks behind the bar to look around. Finds a pistol. A noise startles him. He puts the pistol back and hurries away from the bar. Mullen enters from the rear with a heavy case of supplies which he places behind the bar with a loud thud.]

MULLEN

  I ain't pouring drinks yet. Not 'til I haul in me boxes.

MORRISSEY

  I'll wait then and watch the street. Quite a neighborhood you got here, Boss, especially with them gypsy parlors up the block. Ever had your future told?

MULLEN

  No, but I been thinking lately about giving it a try. You see coppers walk into your saloon and arrest one of your mates, it has a way of shaking you up.

MORRISSEY

Goes to show that even the best of shovers can end up in the wrong place at the wrong time. How about you, Boss? Ever try your hand at the coney business?

MULLEN

You seem to be making the assumption that Terrance Mullen is a crooked man.

MORRISSEY

Just wondering if you had the chance to earn yourself some easy money.

[Mullen suddenly grabs him.]

MULLEN

Now you listen to me, paddy, and listen good. This saloon is open to anyone wants to come in here, and that includes coney men, thieves, and thugs a lot worse than them. I don't care who they are or what they done, as long as they got the nickels in their pockets to pay for their drinks, and the sense in their heads not to disturb the peace. So, do me the favor of not judging me by the customers I serve. I am at heart an honest man trying to run a business in a poor neighborhood.

[Morrissey pulls free, points to the bust of Lincoln behind the bar.]

MORRISSEY

Is that why you got that statue? To remind us you're an honest man?

MULLEN

That thing was there when we opened the place, Cornelius and me. And I know the boys make fun of it. They find it peculiar to look up from their beer and find Abraham Lincoln staring down at them, but that ain't what I find peculiar.

MORRISSEY
You referring to Miss Bridgette the snake?

MULLEN
I'm referring to the bad luck what brought them coppers here. It's peculiar that such misfortune would arise so soon after a fella from Wicklow walked through that door with the address of me saloon in his pocket and the name of Jack Hughes on his tongue.

[Mullen glares at Morrissey and exits to the rear. Once he is gone, Morrissey sneaks behind the bar again to look around. Hughes enters from the street and watches him for a moment.]

HUGHES
Does Mullen know you help yourself to his liquor when he ain't around?

MORRISSEY
His liquor? Oh. No, sir, but I, um, I am planning to pay him for it.

HUGHES
Why in the bleeding hell would you want to do that? Bottom cabinet, top shelf. That's where he hides the Jameson. Pour us a couple of tall ones.

MORRISSEY
Steal his whiskey?

HUGHES
We ain't stealing his whiskey. We're letting the house buy us a drink.

MORRISSEY
[Sets up two whiskeys.] Mr. Hughes, I thought you was in jail.

HUGHES
That I was, lad. In jail. Out of jail. That's how it works when you got a smart lawyer.

MORRISSEY
So, they dropped the charges against you?

HUGHES
No, it's out on bail they got me. I have a trial yet to do. If I'm still in the neighborhood. But for now, what I need is that whiskey. Make it taller, lad. I got me an awful thirst.

MORRISSEY
Here's to you, Mr. Hughes! Or should I still be calling you Shepherd?

HUGHES
Call me Jack. It's a lot easier. Slainte!

[They toast and drink.]

Now put everything back and get out from there quick! Trouble's coming!

[Morrissey does so. Mullen enters with another case.]

MULLEN
Look at this now. Out of the brambles already and without a scratch to show for it. What did it cost this time?

HUGHES
Two thousand, but it was Nelson paid most of it.

MULLEN
What do you say, Morrissey, is a scraggly shover like this worth two thousand dollars?

HUGHES
The judge thought I was worth three. Now is this a drinking saloon or a temperance society? You got customers here dying of thirst.

MULLEN

You'll have to keep dying 'til I'm done with me boxes. Welcome back, Jack.

[Mullen gives him a nod and exits to the rear.]

MORRISSEY

You gonna tell Mullen you seen me behind his bar?

HUGHES

You gonna tell him I know where he hides the Jameson?

MORRISSEY

Then I guess we got an understanding, you and me.

HUGHES

If you show me that letter from Frenchy the Burglar, we do. You still got that letter?

[Morrissey hands him a letter.]

MORRISSEY

Here you go, Jack. Feast your eyes!

HUGHES

Well, me, oh my! Yes, sir, this is one good-looking letter. The way he writes the words, it's a work of art, is what it is. What's it say here at the bottom?

MORRISSEY

"To money, friendship, and money! Your pal, Frenchy." Can you not read it, Jack?

HUGHES

Never went in for all that reading and writing they shove down your throat. But that's okay. I don't want to read your personal letter. Just wanted to see it. Something from Frenchy the Burglar himself! You must be quite the lad to have friends like that!

[Mullen hauls in another heavy case.]

MULLEN
It's bloody roasting hot out there and it stinks in the alley like a dead cat. You jokers should be grateful you ain't in the saloon business.

[He sneers at Morrissey and exits to the rear.]

MORRISSEY
After all these weeks, he still treats me like a mongrel waiting to bite his leg.

HUGHES
I'll tell you what to do then. Bring 'round some of your famous friends. When Mullen sees the company you keep, he'll start treating you with proper respect.

MORRISSEY
I just want to break into the coney trade, is all.

HUGHES
You're a horse thief. Why in hell would you want to be a coney man?

MORRISSEY
Horse stealing is a lousy business. I been shot at by farmers, bitten by dogs, hunted by marshals and vigilance men. Everybody hates horse thieves, and I'll tell you why. You stole someone's horse? You didn't just take away their means of getting around. For most of 'em, you have also just snatched the member of their family that they love most.

HUGHES
The money must be awfully good, though.

MORRISSEY
Nah, you got to travel fifty miles before it's safe to sell a horse what's stolen. Even then you better sell it quick

and that means selling it cheap. I still get nightmares about horses.

[Mullen hauls in another heavy case.]

MULLEN
All right, this is it. Me boxes are in and me saloon is open. You each want your usual?

HUGHES
Today I'm in the mood for something different, so I believe I'll have his usual.

MORRISSEY
In that case, I believe I'll have his.

[Mullen sneers at them both and pours drinks.]

Scene VII

[The Hub a few weeks later. The gang inspects paper bills which they quickly hide as Morrissey enters from the street.]

HUGHES

If it ain't himself coming through the door, at last, and with the Devil's grin on his face!

NELSON

Morrissey, where've you been all week? We thought you fell into some hot water you couldn't climb out of.

MORRISSEY

Ain't no such water. Anybody been here for me yet? I'm expecting me famous pal Billy Brown.

HUGHES

Is that Billy Brown the famous burglar you'd be referring to?

MORRISSEY

Yes, sir. One of me most famous friends of all. And look at that, here he comes now!

[Nealy enters as "Billy Brown." He's nervous.]

This is him, me pal, Billy Brown. Well, Billy?

NEALY AS "BILLY BROWN"
[*Looks around.*] It's good news.

MORRISSEY
How good?

BILLY BROWN
Mighty good. Shall we step outside for a minute?

MORRISSEY
No need for that. These are me pals.

BILLY BROWN
You sure you want to do this here?

MORRISSEY
Come on, Billy, show me what you got while the sun's
still shining.

BILLY BROWN
This is your share. Sixty dollars. I have to go now.

MORRISSEY
Hold on. Sixty dollars! This calls for whiskey!

BILLY BROWN
No, I got a job to do with Smiling Mike. And he won't
be smiling if I shows up late.

[*Billy Brown looks around nervously and exits.*]

MORRISSEY
That's Billy Brown for you. A professional man from
head to toe!

HUGHES
Jesus, Mary, and Joseph! If that's coney, it's the best
damned stuff I ever seen!

MORRISSEY
This ain't coney, Jack. It's the real thing, the nails and
the putty!

MULLEN

What the hell did you fellas do, rob a bank?

MORRISSEY

No, sir, a tannery up in Waukegan. Helped ourselves to a first-class pile of leather, then took it down to Billy's brother in Michigan City to sell it for us.

HUGHES

Ah, money! Ain't it beautiful? Like something what fell out of Heaven itself!

MULLEN

Nelson, we need to talk.

[Mullen exits to the rear. Nelson follows.]

MORRISSEY

What's going on?

HUGHES

Did you not notice the look on Mullen's face? I been telling him what a grand lad you are and he finally seen it for himself. Sure, it's mighty impressed you got all of us now.

MORRISSEY

Then teach me the coney trade. I'm a fast learner and have an ability to remember things.

HUGHES

I know you're a bright one, lad, but this ain't the time to be breaking into the coney business. And here's why. *[Lays out two five-dollar bills.]* Look careful now at these two fivers and tell me which is queer.

MORRISSEY

It's easy to see when you lay them side by side. This one is real. That one is queer. You can tell by them people. On the queer one, they looks like they're under water.

HUGHES
You're right about the people, but your answer is still wrong.

MORRISSEY
How could that be a real fiver?

HUGHES
It ain't real, and neither is this one. They're both queer. The difference is, that pitiful piece of shite is the work of the engraver we're stuck with now. And this beauty here is the work of none other than Mr. Benjamin Boyd. Ever hear of Ben Boyd?

MORRISSEY
No, sir, but this is first-class coney. You got more of these?

HUGHES
Not since Ben Boyd went to prison. Breaks me heart. The world's best engraver of counterfeit plates – the king of coney himself – sitting behind bars with no way to exercise the talents God gave him. What's worse, he ain't due out for ten years!

MORRISSEY
There must be some decent coney somewhere. All we need to do is find it.

HUGHES
No, what we need to do is get Ben Boyd out of prison!

[Mullen and Nelson return from the rear.]

MULLEN
Everyone have a seat. It's time for a meeting.

MORRISSEY
Something wrong, Boss?

MULLEN

We can't have a proper meeting unless everyone is seated.

[Waits for the others to sit. Then he sits and assumes an official pose.]

What we're about to discuss is between us. No one else – not even your mother if you still got a mother – may know of it. Do you swear, Morrissey, to keep this secret?

MORRISSEY

Yes, sir.

MULLEN

Given the sorry state of the coney business, we've been having certain discussions in recent days about how to rise above our lot in life. After much deliberation, and so on and so forth, we finally settled on one idea that we think holds promise.

NELSON

We didn't at first. In fact, we couldn't believe we were even considering this idea at all, being that it is of a dark and unusual nature.

MULLEN

But it kept coming up again. And the more we thought on it, the more we found this one idea to be interesting. Then it occurred to us that you also might find it interesting.

HUGHES

What he's trying to say is, we'd like you to come in on a job with us.

MORRISSEY

But it ain't coney we're talking about?

MULLEN

No, mate, it's a man in Wisconsin named King who, we been told, is filthy rich.

NELSON

Or was filthy rich. He recently passed away and now lies six feet under in a bone orchard in Kenosha.

MULLEN

The point is that dead men don't need money and living men do. So, we been asking ourselves. What if the dearly departed Mr. King was to disappear one night from his grave? Would his grieving loved ones not pay a handsome reward for his return?

MORRISSEY

You want to steal the man's body?

MULLEN

No, mate, we want to kidnap the man's body and then, for a certain price, return it. We think a body like that, a rich man's body, could fetch as much as a thousand dollars.

HUGHES

A delicious pie that cuts up nicely for four hungry men with empty plates. In other words, two hundred and fifty dollars each!

MULLEN

Are you good at digging things up, mate?

MORRISSEY

That I am, sir. And, well, if the truth were to be told, it wouldn't be the first time I done such digging.

NELSON

You've been a grave robber before?

MORRISSEY

Them in the trade prefer to be called "resurrectionists." Before I went to Nebraska, I made good money at it right here in Chicago resurrecting bodies and selling them to medical schools. All in the name of science, of course.

HUGHES

Well, lad, it looks like we're gonna be partners after all!

MORRISSEY

Not so fast, Jack. You get caught snatching a body in Illinois, it's only a few months in jail. But the law in Wisconsin could be different. I need to see if it's worth the risk.

MULLEN

I'll hand it to you, Morrissey, you're a far cry sharper than I expected.

MORRISSEY

Just had a little experience in the resurrection business, is all. Back in the old days, they all knew who I was. The medical schools. The other resurrectionists. They used to have a name for me back then. They used to call me "the boss body snatcher of Chicago."

Scene VIII

[The Hub a week later. Late at night. Hughes and Mullen sit at the table with drinks.]

MORRISSEY

I keep having this dream. I'm all alone in a big prairie and I can hear a storm coming. The rumble of thunder. Only it ain't a storm I discover as I turn about. It's a stampede of horses coming at me. Kicking up clouds of dust so thick it's turning the sky black. Then that rumbling gets so loud, it's roaring in me ears and the earth is shaking under me feet like all the world is coming to an end. I want to run, but ain't no place to run to. While them horses keep coming at me, closer and closer, 'til finally I can see the fire in their eyes, and I know now this is it. I'm gonna be trampled into the ground by all them horses, all them galloping hooves, and, once they're done, won't nothing be left of me. Nothing but dust blowing in the wind. That's when I wake up. And there I am, all alone again.

[Nelson enters from the street.]

NELSON

Tomorrow night is the full moon. A grand light for digging in the dark! How about it, Morrissey? Have you a sturdy shovel?

HUGHES

He won't be needing no shovel. The lad has turned us down.

MORRISSEY

In Wisconsin, you get caught robbing a grave, they put you in prison for two years. Now for one what just got out of prison, a share of that thousand dollars ain't worth the risk of being locked up again for so long. Sorry to decline your offer, but—

[Mullen has entered form the rear.]

MULLEN

Hold on, mate. What if it was a larger sum we was dividing up? Might that rekindle your interest in working with us?

MORRISSEY

That would depend on how much larger that particular sum would be.

MULLEN

What if, instead of a thousand dollars, it was a hundred thousand?

MORRISSEY

A hundred thousand dollars?

HUGHES

Picture it, lad. A mountain of money stacked up on this table, and us sitting here like fat bankers dividing it all up while we're sipping our French champagne!

MULLEN

What would you be willing to do for a chop at that hundred thousand?

MORRISSEY

For that amount, I might do anything, but it's idle thinking, is it not? I see no mountain of money coming to The Hub.

MULLEN

That ain't what the fortune teller says from the parlor up the street.

MORRISSEY

What the hell would bring in a hundred thousand dollars?

NELSON

That which is most valuable to the State of Illinois.

HUGHES

So valuable that the State of Illinois would not only pay one hundred thousand dollars for it, but also release Ben Boyd from prison. Then he could get back to making them beautiful plates and we'd all start getting decent coney again.

MORRISSEY

So, we ain't talking no more about a dead man in Kenosha.

NELSON

We made up the story about Mr. King. We figured that, if you weren't being solid with us, you'd tell others about it and there'd be rumors up and down the street. But we checked around, and there are no such rumors.

MORRISSEY

I see. It ain't no mountain of money I smell here at The Hub. It's a mountain of mistrust.

MULLEN

Don't get sore, mate. When you hear how big this plan is, you'll understand why we had to take precautions before we could tell you about it.

MORRISSEY
Then tell me now. What is the thing most valuable to the State of Illinois?

NELSON
You'll find it down in Springfield at the Oak Ridge Cemetery.

MORRISSEY
We're still talking about graveyards?

MULLEN
Aye, mate, it's why we need you with us. You're shrewd and practiced in matters where we got no experience. And we can't make no mistakes. Not with something this big.

MORRISSEY
What's so valuable at the Oak Ridge Cemetery?

HUGHES
You need to brush up on your history, lad. That's where the Lincoln Monument is.

MORRISSEY
You want to steal the Lincoln Monument?

MULLEN
No, mate. We want to steal the fella what's buried inside it.

[He motions to the bust of Lincoln behind the bar.]

Scene IX

[*Tyrrell and Swegles in the Secret Service office the next day.*]

TYRRELL

Steal Abraham Lincoln? [*Silence. Studies him.*] Okay, how much have you had to drink?

SWEGLES

I ain't been drinking, sir. I been roping. And it's Mr. Lincoln's body they're after.

TYRRELL

Are you sure this isn't another strange game they're playing to test your loyalty?

SWEGLES

This time it's for real, sir. I can tell by the fear in their eyes when they talk about it.

[*Silence. Tyrrell stares off.*]

Captain Tyrrell, are you all right?

TYRRELL

How could any human being be so foul as to conceive such a horrible act?

SWEGLES

I don't know, sir. How soon will you be having these men arrested?

[Silence. Tyrrell stares off.]

Captain Tyrrell?

TYRRELL

Sorry, I need a minute here. Haven't got a word to say that makes a lick of sense.

SWEGLES

I understand, sir. It's the kind of news that has a way of punching you in the face.

TYRRELL

This is the Great Emancipator we're talking about. I must send a telegram to Washington.

SWEGLES

What about arresting these fellas at The Hub before they get any further?

TYRRELL

Arrest them for what? We have no evidence of a crime.

SWEGLES

To let them continue, sir, it would be the most damnable thing.

TYRRELL

It is an unfortunate fact of life that sometimes we must be damnable.

SWEGLES

I'm palling around with men who chat over their beers about using corpses to get rich. How much more damnable do you want me to get?

TYRRELL
We need legal evidence of what these miscreants wish to do. To acquire that evidence, I'm afraid we will have to let them get dangerously close to doing it. *[Studies him for a moment.]* You have the unfortunate look of a man who is about to quit his job.

SWEGLES
It ain't quitting I have in mind, sir. It's getting put on another case, is all.

TYRRELL
And what the hell am I supposed to do with this case? Look, Lewis, if you want to do something important in your life, the time has come. You have been called by Fate and the United States Secret Service to protect the legacy of Abraham Lincoln.

SWEGLES
Working on a case of such magnitude, would it be worth more than five dollars a day?

TYRRELL
Far more, but not in dollars and cents. This is a chance to be a hero. To do something that will be remembered for years to come. Do you believe in the afterlife?

SWEGLES
No, sir.

TYRRELL
Neither did President Lincoln. For him, the key to immortality was to do great deeds during his time here on earth. He believed that, if you accomplish things that will be remembered, you can live forever in the minds and hearts of others.

SWEGLES
So, it's immortality that you're offering.

TYRRELL

[Holds up a five-dollar bill.] Immortality and five dollars a day.

SWEGLES

If I succeed, will people be told this time about what I done?

TYRRELL

If you wish. But I must warn you that stepping out of the shadows and into the light would come at a cost. You would no longer be able to work undercover.

SWEGLES

I want my name in the newspaper for something other than stealing horses.

[He reaches over and takes the money.]

Scene X

[The Hub a week later. Late at night. Mullen, Hughes, and Morrissey are seated at the table.]

MULLEN

This is what's known as a planning session.

MORRISSEY

Shouldn't we wait for Nelson?

MULLEN

Nelson is on the train to Springfield to see what he can learn about the monument. He'll report back in two days. Which is when we'll have our next planning session.

HUGHES

Before we start this one, I'd like to say that I believe we could get more money.

MORRISSEY

More than a hundred thousand?

HUGHES

A man like Abraham Lincoln has got to be worth at least a hundred and twenty-five thousand. That's twenty-five thousand apiece after we divide the money five ways.

MORRISSEY

Wait a minute. I thought we was dividing the money four ways. Us three and Nelson.

HUGHES

We can't forget Cornelius. He's the man in charge.

MULLEN

Just a damned minute now. Cornelius ain't the "man in charge."

HUGHES

What else do you call it when you order everyone around and don't do nothing yourself?

MULLEN

Cornelius is the one who hatched this idea. That makes him a smart thinker. But it don't make him the "man in charge."

MORRISSEY

Will he be doing the work along with us?

MULLEN

Cornelius is a busy man what don't wish to be involved in the details of stealing the body. He also likes to stay out of view. That's why you ain't gonna meet him.

MORRISSEY

I'm to share all that money with somebody I'll never see?

MULLEN

Exactly right, mate. In the meantime, I have to agree with Hughes. A hundred thousand ain't enough. Not for "the" Mr. Lincoln himself.

HUGHES

Then it's settled. We'll ask for a hundred and twenty-five thousand.

MULLEN

No. We'll ask for a hundred and fifty thousand. That will give us thirty thousand each.

HUGHES

I wonder what Cornelius will say about this.

MULLEN

He'll be happy as a clam at high tide when we're all basking in the glow of our wealth.

HUGHES

You'll be basking without me, because I meself will be back in Ireland then.

MULLEN

What the bloody hell would you be doing in Ireland?

HUGHES

Getting away from the cops in Chicago. I'll take a trip to Cork to see me poor old mammy and give her a slice of that loot so she can buy herself some knickknacks for the house. Or maybe we'll just buy a new house. What the hell. We'll have the money for it!

MORRISSEY

That's mighty generous of you, Jack, to be thinking of your mam now.

HUGHES

I'm also thinking about a certain Connie O'Connor on whom I might pay a visit if she ain't married by now. Or even if she is, I could still drop by. Rich men can do whatever they please. So, I'll bring her roses like I used to. But big ones this time and lots of 'em. D'you know that women find rich men to be extremely attractive?

MULLEN

You ain't got no money yet. So, if you want a ticket to

that Emerald Isle, you'd better start coming up with some ideas for getting into that damned tomb.

MORRISSEY

Of all the tombs in the world, this must be the hardest to break into.

MULLEN

Cornelius says it will be easy because nobody will be expecting it. Who the hell would try to steal the body of Abraham Lincoln?

HUGHES

Cornelius is right. We got the element of surprise on our side.

MORRISSEY

Suppose we do get Mr. Lincoln's body. Every lawman in Illinois will be looking for it.

MULLEN

That's why we'll use one of Nelson's freight wagons to move the body up to the sand dunes of Indiana. It's there we'll plant old Lincoln while we wait for the money.

HUGHES

Because the beauty of the sand dunes is that they never stop moving in the wind. Within hours of our digging, all signs of what we done, even our footsteps, will be gone!

MULLEN

That was an elegant idea, if I don't say so meself.

HUGHES

You make it sound like it was you what thought it up.

MULLEN

It was me what thought it up. Cornelius wanted to bury the body by the Sangamom River. I said, "No, that's too close to the scene of the crime. And who wants to dig in the dark by a damned river? Too many little slimy things crawling around in unexpected places."

HUGHES
That's when I said, "Let's bring the body up north."

MULLEN
Yes, but "bringing the body up north" don't mean bringing the body "to the Indiana dunes." It means bringing the body "up north."

HUGHES
All right, Jimmy Boy, where are the Indiana dunes located in relationship to Springfield?

MORRISSEY
I guess they would be "up north."

MULLEN
A lot of places is "up north" in relationship to Springfield! The North Pole is "up north" in relationship to Springfield! You said "up north" and I said "the dunes."

HUGHES
Watch out for him, lad. He's always trying to steal your glory.

MULLEN
I know what I know and I am what I am. Now back to business. We still got to decide when to steal the body. First week of December is when we'll do it.

HUGHES
That's four weeks. If we wait that long, we could find ourselves in the snow and ice. Now I don't mind digging sand, but I don't like digging snow.

MULLEN
We can't just up and go to Abraham Lincoln's tomb. We need a plan.

HUGHES
We got all the plan we need, except for the particulars of how to get into the tomb. And we'll know about that when Nelson returns from Oak Ridge.

MULLEN
We still ain't decided how to ask for the money. Cornelius thinks it should be Ben Boyd himself what negotiates with the government.

MORRISSEY
Does Ben Boyd get a cut of the money as well?

HUGHES
No, he gets out of jail, is what he gets. Then he can make his own money.

MULLEN
But too many things can go wrong when you got prison guards between you and your spokesman. So, it shall be meself what goes to the government and asks for the loot.

MORRISSEY
What will stop them from arresting you?

MULLEN
The belief that I am an innocent bystander what has been forced by the kidnappers to speak on their behalf. I will be regarded not as a crook, but as a public benefactor.

MORRISSEY
Why would the government believe anything you say?

HUGHES
He's got a good point.

MULLEN
This is why we need you, Morrissey. Counterfeiters are idea men. They can think things up easy enough.

But sometimes they need a good thief to help them work out the details.

Scene XI

[The Hub two days later. Late at night. Morrissey drinks while Mullen works behind the bar.]

MORRISSEY
  There must be some way I could meet Cornelius.

MULLEN
  It's too late now. He's back in St. Louis.

MORRISSEY
  So, he's from St. Louis, is he? *[Silence.]* What kind of fella would come up with the idea of stealing Abraham Lincoln?

MULLEN
  This ain't the first time the idea got thought. According to Big Jim, there was a strange lawyer in Springfield had a similar notion ten years ago, but nothing never come of it.

MORRISSEY
  Who's Big Jim?

MULLEN
  What?

MORRISSEY

You said it was Big Jim what told you about the strange lawyer in Springfield.

MULLEN

All right, I shouldn't be saying this, but what the hell. "Big Jim" is the real name of the man we usually refer to as "Cornelius."

MORRISSEY

I know a fella from St. Louis named Big Jim Duffy. That wouldn't be him, would it?

MULLEN

His name ain't Duffy, it's Kennally. Okay, I probably shouldn't of said that neither.

MORRISSEY

Knowing his real name ain't gonna change nothing when it comes time to resurrect Mr. Lincoln, though it is disappointing to learn we ain't the first ones in history to plan it.

MULLEN

I've got news for you, mate. We ain't the second ones neither.

MORRISSEY

You make it sound like people try this all the time.

MULLEN

Only one other time I know of. It was Big Jim Kennally himself what led the effort with a gang of coney men from Logan County, but nothing never come of that neither.

MORRISSEY

If it's been shown the idea don't work, why the hell are we trying it again?

MULLEN

It ain't the idea what was the problem. It was the people. A bunch of jokers, they was.

MORRISSEY

So, they never actually went into the tomb?

MULLEN

They never actually done nothing but sit around and drink.

[A banging at the door. Mullen unlocks it and lets in Nelson.]

NELSON

I thought we were having a meeting. Where's Jack?

MORRISSEY

He ain't here yet.

NELSON

If we can't even start a meeting on time, how the hell are we going to commit the crime of the century? That's what this would be, you know. The crime of the century!

MULLEN

Nelson, is something wrong?

NELSON

The monument. It's one hell of a solid-looking pile. My God, what on earth led us to believe that we could march in there, grab the body of Abraham Lincoln, and march out with it like a stolen pie from a window sill.

MULLEN

This ain't exactly the news we've been waiting to hear.

NELSON

It's the news you're getting. And, if you do proceed with this morbid plan, it will not be one of my freight wagons you use.

MORRISSEY
How will we transport the body?

NELSON
All I know is, I can't risk my business and family by having my wagons involved.

MORRISSEY
So, you're quitting us then?

NELSON
No, but henceforth I shall need to remain more in the background. Like Cornelius.

MULLEN
You can refer to him as "Big Jim" now. We all know who he is.

NELSON
Is Big Jim aware that we all know who he is?

MULLEN
What the hell cares? Now tell us about this tomb.

NELSON
When you arrive at Oak Ridge, you suddenly find it looming in front of you, the Lincoln Monument! Did you know it cost two hundred thousand dollars?

MULLEN
Very nice! They must have a lot of money down there!

NELSON
How in God's name would we ever break into a two hundred-thousand-dollar monument?

MORRISSEY
There has to be some way to get into that tomb.

NELSON
There's a door, of course, but they keep it locked. It's

made it of iron rods so you can look through and see the
sarcophagus.

MULLEN

Big Jim thinks it'll be easy to break through that iron
door. Did it seem that way to you?

NELSON

I don't know. I was looking at the sarcophagus. Fancy
marble, it's made of, with an inscription on the end plate.
"With malice toward none. With charity toward all."

[They look at one another anxiously.]

MORRISSEY

How many guards do they have at night to watch the
tomb?

NELSON

I didn't ask. Why would a cemetery visitor want to know
something like that?

MULLEN

So, you went all the bloody way down there and you
learned nothing.

NELSON

I learned more than I expected, and I'm grateful to God
for it.

MULLEN

Say what you will. I ain't gonna be scared off by a few
words in a bloody tomb.

NELSON

It is Abraham Lincoln's tomb! And those words are from
his last inaugural address!

MULLEN

I don't give a fiddler's fart where them words is from.

Not when there's a hundred and fifty thousand dollars involved!

NELSON

A hundred and fifty thousand?

MORRISSEY

We raised the price.

[A banging at the door. Mullen unlocks it and lets in Hughes.]

HUGHES

I'm coming with bad news. It ain't even so much as a penny she'll give us.

MORRISSEY

Jack, who have you been telling about our plan?

MULLEN

Allie Boyd. That's Ben Boyd's wife. We figured that, since we're going to all this trouble to free her husband, she should be willing to cover our expenses.

HUGHES

She don't want nothing to do with it. She don't even want us to use Ben Boyd's name.

MORRISSEY

How are we supposed to free him from prison if we don't use his name?

HUGHES

She don't want him free from prison.

MULLEN

We'll worry about the money later. Everyone sit down so we can have a proper meeting.

[They all sit at the table.]

We shall now discuss the sarcophagus and what's in it.

HUGHES
Jesus, Mary, and Joseph, we all know what's in it. That's why we're doing this!

MULLEN
But what do you see exactly when you open it? Old Man Lincoln staring up at you?

NELSON
No, if you open the sarcophagus, I believe you would see not him, but his casket.

MULLEN
Do we steal the whole works? Or do we take only the body and leave the casket behind?

MORRISSEY
If we took only the body, how would we carry it?

HUGHES
We could always put it in a sack.

NELSON
No! You cannot put Abraham Lincoln in a sack!

MORRISSEY
Nelson's right. It's too disrespectful. Besides, we don't want to damage the corpse.

MULLEN
All right, if the old man is still in his casket, we'll keep him in there and shoulder it out.

HUGHES
Will there be a smell?

MULLEN
He's been dead for eleven years. That's got to smell like something.

HUGHES
I hadn't really thought about the smell.

NELSON
There is a lot you haven't thought about this: monstrous idea, what it entails, and whether it's worth any amount of money in the world!

[Mullen smashes the table. The others leap away.]

MULLEN
Keep that up, Nelson, and it won't be the table I'm smashing. What's got into you?

NELSON
Some people might call it a sense of decency!

[Nelson storms out and slams the door.]

MORRISSEY
Now what?

MULLEN
We need another man.

Scene XII

[The Hub a few nights later. Nealy sits nervously at a table. Swegles as "Morrissey" paces.]

NEALY

I can't believe I'm doing this.

MORRISSEY

Try to remember that you're a patriot acting for the good of his country.

NEALY

By cavorting with ghouls?

MORRISSEY

By helping the Secret Service protect the body of Abraham Lincoln.

NEALY

Lewis, it's just you and me now. You can drop the counterfeit brogue.

MORRISSEY

No, it's too confusing if I do. And me name ain't Lewis. It's Morrissey.

NEALY

Either way, I ain't placing one toe inside the tomb of Abraham Lincoln. And I don't care how much your creepy detective friend tries to pay me. Oh, my Lord, I feel like I'm gonna faint.

MORRISSEY

Come on, Nealy, you knew what you was getting into when you agreed to do this.

NEALY

But meeting body snatchers face to face makes it all the more gruesome. That's what we are engaged in here. A gruesome endeavor.

MORRISSEY

Look, I don't want to be here no more than you do.

NEALY

That ain't what I see. I've known you a long time, Lewis. Ever since you was a young tar getting your sea legs. And I can tell something about you has changed. The way you pal around with these ghouls. It seems awful easy.

MORRISSEY

That's how it's supposed to seem. I'm a roper now. And so are you for the time being.

NEALY

[Pause. Thinks about it.] I can't believe I'm doing this.

MORRISSEY

Look, you're a good roper. You got a talent for talking crooked. And they like you. I can tell. They think you're a first-class burglar.

NEALY

I still say they're ghouls.

MORRISSEY

Mullen is the one to worry about. Hughes ain't so bad underneath it all.

NEALY

Ain't that comforting. What are they doing back there anyway, chopping up bodies?

MORRISSEY

I don't know, but you'd better be ready for them when they come back out.

NEALY

All right then. I ain't William Nealy. I'm Billy Brown. I ain't straight. I'm crooked. And this ain't the strangest and most unbelievable fecking thing I ever done in me life.

MORRISSEY

That's the way now. All you have to do is pretend.

NEALY

Where I'm from, they don't call it pretending. They call it lying. Them that tell too many lies end up in the part of Hell where you can't tell your arse from the hole it's stuck in.

MORRISSEY

Never mind about that. We got grave robbers to contend with.

NEALY

Then tell me this, Mr. Secret Service Man. How long would it take for a rig to go from Springfield, Illinois, to the dunes of Indiana?

MORRISSEY

 A day or two, I suppose.

NEALY

As a hack driver, I can tell you that it'll take ten days if the roads is bad. That's ten days and ten nights with the stolen body of Abraham Lincoln in the back of the cart. And they think nobody will notice?

MORRISSEY

It don't matter. They'll never get nowhere close to doing that.

NEALY

But it's what they're planning. These are stupid men! And there's nothing more dangerous than stupid men who think they've got a great idea!

[The rear door opens. Mullen and Hughes enter. Everyone looks at everyone else. They all sit.]

MULLEN

Okay, Billy Brown, we welcome you to our enterprise. And, though you are coming into it late, we wish to be generous. We will divide up the loot, therefore, so you get almost nearly as much as everyone else, almost.

MORRISSEY

Don't worry. He'll earn every dollar.

MULLEN

We know he will, mate. And, speaking of money, we did learn that the Lincoln Monument is worth two hundred thousand dollars. The question we had to ask was—

HUGHES

What is the use of the monument without the corpse?

MULLEN

That's why we've raised the asking price to two hundred thousand. The government will gladly pay it. Without the body, their monument would be worthless.

HUGHES

As the only one here what's facing a trial, I also wish to

demand my freedom. The State of Illinois must drop all counterfeiting charges against me. Any objections?

MORRISSEY
It's fine with me, Jack.

MULLEN
Fine with me, too.

NEALY AS ""BILLY BROWN"
No problem.

MULLEN
Billy, we're glad you could join us. We like it that you ain't only a hack driver, but also a cracksman what knows his way around stone. What if the lid of this sarcophagus was too heavy to lift. What would you do?

BILLY BROWN
Drill a hole in. Pack it with powder. Blow it off.

MORRISSEY
He does this all the time, except it's usually bank vaults and such he's blowing up.

HUGHES
How many banks have you robbed?

BILLY BROWN
Enough to know what I'm doing.

MULLEN
This is a good man. What tools will we need if we have to resort to drilling and blasting?

BILLY BROWN
A can of powder. A fathom of fuse. A hammer.

MORRISSEY
Some steel punch drills. Maybe a steel file.

HUGHES

With you lads along, we'll be in and out of that stinking tomb in the bat of an eye.

BILLY BROWN

[With a knowing glance at Morrissey.] Yeah, then all we have to do is drive that old casket up to the Indiana dunes.

MULLEN

Except that, with Nelson gone, we lost our rig. And we ain't got no money to hire one.

BILLY BROWN

No problem. When we get to Springfield, I'll steal one.

MULLEN

That's what you're in charge of, mate. Drilling, Blasting, and Transportation.

MORRISSEY

This must be the first kidnapping in history where the victim is already dead.

MULLEN

That's why we got to plan it all out. That reminds me. I got something to show you. *[Gets out a newspaper.]* The Catholic Union and Times. This is how I, the innocent bystander, will prove to the government that I been forced be you, the kidnappers, to speak on your behalf.

MORRISSEY

With a newspaper?

MULLEN

Published in London and Dublin but so rare in this part of the world that the only place I know to find it is at Tom Mankin's newsstand on Dearborn. Watch careful now. *[Rips a page diagonally in two.]* We will take this half of the page with us to Springfield and leave it in the sarcophagus. The coppers will know it's a message from the kidnappers. Why? Because such a rare newspaper could be not be lying in the sarcophagus, tore in half, by accident. *[Holds up the other half of the page.]* When it's time to go to the government, I will show them this half of the page. They will see it fits the other half perfectly. And they will know that I am their man. Morrissey?

MORRISSEY
Good idea.

MULLEN
Billy Brown?

BILLY BROWN
Good idea.

[Mullen looks at Hughes, who shrugs.]

HUGHES
It's good enough, I suppose, if we can't come up with nothing better.

MORRISSEY
[Reading newspaper.] Look. They got a story here about the election. It says that, with Tilden running against Hayes, it could lead to the Civil War all over again.

MULLEN
That's enough now. This ain't a newspaper to be read. It is a tool to be used in a kidnapping operation. Speaking of which, we still need to decide what day to strike. Let's ponder it, mates. When would four men like us be least likely to be noticed?

[Silence. They look at one another uncertainly.]

MORRISSEY
Wait. The answer is right here in this newspaper. Tuesday is when we should strike.

HUGHES

What's so special about Tuesday?

MORRISSEY

It's November seventh, Election day! The streets of downtown Springfield will be packed with voters and, at night, they'll all be in the saloons waiting to see who won.

HUGHES

The lad is right. No one will be at the monument then.

BILLY BROWN

Sounds like Tuesday might be a good time to do it.

MULLEN

It is a damned elegant time to do it!

MORRISSEY

It won't be long before this page from the Catholic Union and Times becomes the most important piece of paper in the State of Illinois, if not the whole world.

MULLEN

Then we had best think twice about the piece we keep in Chicago. This is the piece that will establish me authority as a public benefactor. Where shall we hide it?

MORRISSEY

Boss, I got just the spot for it!

[Morrissey takes the newspaper piece and hides it inside the hollow bust of Lincoln behind the bar.]

Well, fellas, what do you say?

HUGHES

I say we leave for Springfield tomorrow!

MORRISSEY AND BILLY BROWN

Aye, tomorrow!

MULLEN
Tomorrow it is then! To Springfield we go to snatch a President!

[With bravado, Mullen takes out his pistol. Morrissey looks anxiously at Billy Brown. Blackout.]

END OF ACT ONE

ACT II

Scene I

[A train platform at night. Swegles as "Morrissey" waits alone in a cloud of steam.]

CONDUCTOR'S VOICE
All aboard for Springfield and St. Louis! All aboard!"

[Tyrrell steps up and looks around cautiously.]

TYRRELL
Where in God's name are Mullen and Hughes?

MORRISSEY
I don't know, sir. We was supposed to meet here by the first car.

TYRRELL
I'm with two Pinkerton detectives at the other end of the platform. We've been waiting for nearly an hour.

MORRISSEY
So, we're all going to Springfield on the same train?

TYRRELL
If Mullen and Hughes ever show up. Might they be on board already?

MORRISSEY
They wasn't when I looked before. Nealy's gone to look again.

TYRRELL
This is ridiculous. Everyone is here but the men we're following.

CONDUCTOR'S VOICE
All aboard for Springfield and St. Louis! All aboard!

[Nealy runs up, out of breath.]

NEALY
They ain't on the train. Maybe they changed their minds.

MORRISSEY
No, they're waiting to the last minute so nobody sees them on the platform.

NEALY
What if they miss the train?

MORRISSEY
They ain't gonna miss the train.

NEALY
I know they ain't, but what if they do? Will I still be getting me five dollars?

TYRRELL
You'll get your five dollars when you have completed your assignment.

NEALY
I'm trying to complete it. I'm here, ain't I?

TYRRELL
Mullen and Hughes must see you board the train. And they must believe that you're going with them to Springfield.

MORRISSEY

Don't worry, sir. He's got it worked out so he can sneak off the train before it even leaves Chicago. Tell him what you're gonna say to the boys after we get on board.

NEALY

"Four men traveling together could prove singular, so I'll be in a sleeper car 'til morning. Then just before Springfield I'll hop off into the countryside to steal a rig. See you tomorrow night at the cemetery, boys, with horses and wagon ready to go!"

MORRISSEY

That's why nobody will be asking where Billy Brown went to.

NEALY

And why I might as well be getting me five dollars now.

TYRRELL

I shall be in the last car with the Pinkertons.

[Tyrrell glares at Nealy and walks off.]

MORRISSEY

Look at you now. Standing here on the night before the night we all been waiting for and all you can think about is your damned money.

NEALY

And I suppose you ain't thinking about yours?

MORRISSEY

I'm thinking about me purpose in life now and what I got to do.

NEALY

Do you know you're still speaking with an Irish accent?

MORRISSEY

Look, I'm doing me best and it ain't easy. So, if you got any other complaints, do me the favor of kindly keeping them to yourself.

NEALY

This purpose in life you got. Is it worth dying for?

MORRISSEY

Now why the hell would you go and say something like that for?

NEALY

This ain't a tiddler's game. These men have guns. Look, Lewis, there's plenty enough heroes in this world. Leave with me tonight and let that horse's ass and his Pinkertons do the rest.

MORRISSEY

I have to protect Abraham Lincoln.

NEALY

Since when did you become so grand that it's you of all people in the world what has to protect Abraham Lincoln?

MORRISSEY

Ain't you ever wanted to do something that'll be remembered?

NEALY

That ain't for men like us to worry about.

MORRISSEY

Say what you will, I got something to do that's more important than money. Though you do make a good point. What if something happens to me in Springfield?

NEALY

Nothing will happen to you in Springfield if you don't go to Springfield.

MORRISSEY

What if I get killed at the tomb and I go to me own grave with everyone thinking I'm a body snatcher? They could write that up in the newspaper, that I was a body snatcher, and there it would be in black and white for the rest of all time.

NEALY

If it came to all that, they would say in the newspaper that you was a roper.

MORRISSEY

How would they know I was a roper? I ain't got no badge says I'm a roper.

NEALY

Tyrrell would tell them you was working for the government.

MORRISSEY

Oh, would he now.

NEALY

My God, Lewis, do you really think he wouldn't tell people the truth?

MORRISSEY

Would he want the world to know he hired a horse thief to protect Abraham Lincoln?

NEALY

If that's how much you trust Tyrrell, why do you work for him?

MORRISSEY

I ain't working for Tyrrell now. I'm working for Mr. Lincoln. But I need your help.

NEALY

No! I told you from the start, I ain't going to Springfield!

MORRISSEY

I ain't asking you to go to Springfield. I'm asking you to tell people the truth if something happens to me. Tell them I weren't no body snatcher named Jim Morrissey. Tell them I was a roper named Lewis Cass Swegles who was trying to do something good.

NEALY

Why would anyone listen to anything I say?

MORRISSEY

I don't know, but, if things turn bad, Nealy, you have to help me protect me name, what's left of it. As one pal to another, would you do that for me?

NEALY

Look, I could say you're a roper. I could even say you're the Prince of Ropers. But ain't nobody gonna pay no attention to a hack driver from Waukegan what smells of horses.

MORRISSEY

But you'll be a pal and try to help. Come on, Nealy. You're the only one besides Tyrrell knows I'm a roper. Tell me at least you'll try.

NEALY

Shhh! Here they come.

[*The train whistle blows as Mullen and Hughes arrive. Mullen carries a bulky carpetbag.*]

CONDUCTOR'S VOICE

This train is now leaving for Springfield and St. Louis! All aboard!

HUGHES

Let's go, lads. We got a train to catch!

NEALY

It's high time. We thought you got cold feet.

MULLEN

Come now, Billy, you need to have more faith in the feet of them you run with. D'you suppose you could muster up a bit more faith?

NEALY

[Aside to Morrissey.] I'll try.

[The train whistle blows again. The gang rushes off to the train as the engine begins to roar.]

Scene II

[The tomb chamber of the Lincoln Monument the next morning. The iron door is open. Morrissey stands inside, staring at the sarcophagus in awe. An echoing noise startles him. He cautiously inspects the open burial vault in the rear wall. Silence. He returns to the sarcophagus.]

MORRISSEY

Forgive me, Mr. Lincoln, if I seem a bit uneasy. First time ever I been in the company of a President.

[He lays his hand reverently on the sarcophagus. Meanwhile a disapproving John Power appears at the door in a suit and tie, startling him again.]

POWER

We don't normally touch the sarcophagus. Nor do we enter this area without permission.

MORRISSEY

Weren't no one out front to ask and the door was wide open, so I figured—

POWER

This is the final resting place of President Lincoln. You cannot just stroll in!

MORRISSEY

I ain't strolling, sir. I'm looking for Captain Patrick Tyrrell. He said to meet him here.

POWER

You're the man from Chicago?

MORRISSEY

Yes, sir. I'm a bit behind schedule, but—

POWER

I expected someone older.

MORRISSEY

Sir, I've been doing me very best and this, so far, is as old as I been able to get.

[Tyrrell appears outside, counting his paces.]

TYRRELL

...one hundred eighteen, one hundred nineteen, one hundred twenty. *[He sees Morrissey. Checks his watch.]* There you are! I was getting worried.

MORRISSEY

Sorry to be late, sir. I had trouble getting out of the hotel without raising suspicion. Then the streetcar was running slow because of all the voters downtown.

TYRRELL

This is Mr. Power, the custodian. He's been showing me around the monument. Mr. Power, this is Lewis Swegles, the agent who—

MORRISSEY

Sir, didn't we agree you would be addressing me today as "Morrissey"?

TYRRELL

What? Oh. Yes, all right, but I had to introduce you to Mr.—

MORRISSEY

Sir, I been up all night on the train. I'm tired and I'm frayed. If I am to get through this day, I cannot be Lewis Swegles for even one minute. It is a matter of concentration.

TYRRELL

Very well then. Mr. Power, this is Jim Morrissey, one of the grave robbers who will be breaking into your tomb tonight. *[Silence. Power is not amused.]* Have you had a chance to see how the monument is laid out?

MORRISSEY

I seen that it has two rooms. This one and the one out front with the statue. But I couldn't find no passage from there to here.

POWER

The only entrance to the tomb is that door which is normally locked.

MORRISSEY

You'd think they'd put a passage inside. That way, if you was in the statue room and you wanted to visit Mr. Lincoln, you wouldn't have to go out and around to the back door.

POWER

The area in front is not a "statue room." It is a visitor's chamber called Memorial Hall. There is no direct access from there to here. And I am sorry that the Lincoln Monument does not meet your architectural standards.

MORRISSEY

Sir, I'm only trying to get the layout. Is it Memorial Hall on the other side of that wall?

POWER

Immediately behind that wall is a storage area that lies

between the two main chambers and is entered from the other side. That's where we were when you first arrived.

MORRISSEY
Must have been you I heard back there.

TYRRELL
I thought the walls were two feet thick.

POWER
Yes, but because of all the marble in the main chambers, sound often echoes through the monument in unpredictable ways.

TYRRELL
If I had a man behind that wall tonight, could he hear the grave robbers at work?

POWER
It's possible. It's also possible, however, that they could hear him.

TYRRELL
Not if he's in place before they arrive. We shall take our positions at half past six. One man in the storage area and five of us in Memorial Hall with the lights out and the front door locked. We shall then wait with the patience of fishermen to make our catch.

POWER
If the man in the storage area has to wait long, he could grow restless. Should he move about, the sounds of his boots could easily betray him.

TYRRELL
Then the man in the storage area shall not wear boots. He shall wait in his stocking feet.

POWER
The group in Memorial Hall will have the same problem. Footsteps could echo from there to here as well.

TYRRELL

Then no one in Memorial Hall shall wear boots. We shall all wait in our stocking feet.

MORRISSEY

Sir, it will be a cold night to be without boots.

TYRRELL

Then we shall be damned uncomfortable! But we shall also be determined! When these filthy swine have finally opened the sarcophagus—

POWER

Must we really allow them to get that far?

TYRRELL

We need irrefutable evidence of their crime.

POWER

On behalf of the National Lincoln Monument Association, I must express my concern about the possibility of damage to the tomb.

TYRRELL

There will be no damage to the sarcophagus or its contents. Right, Morrissey?

MORRISSEY

Yes, sir. But, when you refer to these men as "filthy swine," I believe you is working against your own purpose in bringing them to justice.

TYRRELL

You think that those who traffic in human remains are not filthy swine?

MORRISSEY

Sir, I ain't defending their actions. I'm only saying that these are ordinary men what have lived their lives in poverty, and now find themselves in desperate straits. To think of them as less than human is to underestimate what they is capable of.

TYRRELL
You sound as if you've developed sympathy for these ghouls.

MORRISSEY
It ain't sympathy so much as understanding. When you got society telling you that you ain't worth shite, and you can't write nor read, and you got no hope of nothing better, it's easy to make bad judgments.

TYRRELL
This is not what I want to hear on the most critical day of our operation. We came to apprehend grave robbers, not plead their case.

POWER
Should we be enlisting the assistance of a different agent?

TYRRELL
No, we must have faith in ourselves and our mission. But we must also be clear about where we stand. Is there anything more you wish to say about Mullen and Hughes?

MORRISSEY
No, sir.

TYRRELL
Then you agree that they are filthy swine who must be separated from decent people.

MORRISSEY
With all due respect, sir, I told you what I believe.

POWER
This is not the man I would have chosen for an assignment of this importance.

TYRRELL

I would like to assure Mr. Power that we are all professionals committed to the success of our mission. May I give Mr. Power that assurance now with full confidence that it is true?

MORRISSEY

Sir, I am standing in the presence of Abraham Lincoln. And I can tell you now that I got one purpose tonight and one purpose only. To protect Mr. Lincoln.

TYRRELL

Then the President's coffin shall not be touched. You have my solemn word on that, Mr. Power. As soon as the lid of the sarcophagus is off, my men and I shall pounce.

POWER

In your stocking feet?

TYRRELL

In whatever state or condition is necessary to arrest these sons of bitches in the act of desecrating Abraham Lincoln's tomb! Isn't that right, Morrissey?

MORRISSEY

Yes, sir.

TYRRELL

Good, because it is you who must let us know when the sarcophagus is open. As soon as that occurs, you will tell the others you are going outside for a cigar. Have you a cigar?

MORRISSEY

No, sir.

TYRRELL

[Takes out a cigar.] Here, take one of mine.

MORRISSEY
Sir, I don't smoke cigars.

TYRRELL
You don't have to smoke the damned thing. Just use it as an excuse to get outside. Then walk around to the front of the monument, step up to the door of Memorial Hall, and give us the password through the opening in the door. The password is "Wash."

POWER
"Wash?" What sort of nonsense is this?

TYRRELL
Sir, we are engaged in serious business that puts all of our lives at risk. "Wash" is short for "Washburn," the former chief of the Secret Service who will be among those with us tonight in Memorial Hall. Once we hear the password, we shall traverse the one hundred and twenty paces from the front of the monument to the back. Our journey will be swift and the thieves shall find themselves under arrest.

POWER
Does Mrs. Lincoln have any idea of what is underway in the tomb of her husband?

TYRRELL
It is the President's son Robert with whom we have been in contact. He knows what we are planning and he has given us his blessing.

POWER
In the name of all that is holy, I cannot imagine a more frightful situation!

TYRRELL
That may be true, but you must remain calm and act normally when the grave robbers arrive this afternoon to request a tour.

POWER

Dear God, no! They're coming for a tour?

TYRRELL

They will pretend to be tourists who have come to visit the Lincoln Monument.

MORRISSEY

Sir, there's been a change of plans. It will be Hughes and meself only what comes to visit this afternoon.

TYRRELL

What's wrong with Mullen?

MORRISSEY

He has grown a bit dejected, sir. He believes that his mustache makes him look crooked and that, if he was to be seen here in the light of day, it might arouse suspicion.

TYRRELL

Very well then, Mr. Power, it may be only Hughes you have to deal with. As custodian, you must give him the same tour you would give anyone else and answer all his questions truthfully. There must be no sign of anything unusual afoot.

POWER

You are asking me to give this body snatcher the information he needs to break in.

TYRRELL

That is, unfortunately, the role you must play. Be prepared to answer questions about the security of the tomb. Or should I say the lack of security.

POWER

The lock on that door has been security enough for years.

TYRRELL

A single padlock is hardly what I would call "security." Your visitor will be delighted to discover that it is the only obstacle standing in his way.

POWER

What if he walks in on us now? We should lock up here and return to Memorial Hall.

MORRISSEY

No need to hurry, sir. The boys will be fast asleep at the St. Charles House until half past ten. Then they plan to have breakfast and tend to some last-minute chores. So, it won't be 'til this afternoon that Mr. Hughes will be ready for the streetcar to Oak Ridge.

POWER

With men of this nature, I don't see how you can be so confident about what they will do.

TYRRELL

It is not only confidence we have to support us. It is two Pinkerton detectives, John McGinn and George Hay, keeping them under surveillance.

POWER

I shall be in Memorial Hall. Be sure to lock the door before you leave.

[POWER storms off.]

TYRRELL

And what, pray tell, are the "last-minute chores" of a grave robber?

MORRISSEY

Jack has a hole in his shoe and wishes to get it repaired. We seen a shop near the hotel where we think he can get it done for a good price.

TYRRELL
[*Studies him for a moment.*] I'm very concerned about you,
Lewis. I shall pray to God you do not let us down.

Scene III

[The tomb entrance that afternoon. The door is now padlocked shut. Morrissey and Hughes peer through the rods of the door as Power stands nearby, as if giving a tour.]

POWER

Mrs. Lincoln wanted to bury the President here so that he would be away from the bustle of the city, but her decision proved to be controversial. A prominent group led by Governor Oglesby wanted to entomb the President in downtown Springfield.

HUGHES

May we go inside for a closer peek?

POWER

I'm sorry, Mr. Smith, the public is not allowed inside the tomb. But feel free to look through the door. After all, this is a tour and you have paid your fee.

HUGHES

It's a crying shame that such a beautiful thing has to be seen through bars.

POWER

I quite agree. And, getting back to Mrs. Lincoln, her wish to bury the President here began with a request he once made to her. They were traveling by carriage—

HUGHES

Excuse me, Mr. Power, but this is so historical a place and it is all the way from Wisconsin we come to see it. Would it be possible to pay an extra fee to step inside?

POWER

Sir, we do not have such fees. They were traveling by carriage through the countryside when they happened upon a cemetery filled with wild flowers.

HUGHES

Suppose it was a private fee. Just between us. How much would it cost for the privilege of stepping inside this magnificent chamber for one or two minutes at the very most?

POWER

This is not a matter of negotiation.

HUGHES

Well, of course not. I didn't think it would be. And I do certainly understand why you'd want to keep the place locked up. His corpse must be worth quite a pretty penny!

MORRISSEY

Not to mention, Mr. Smith, that it's a matter of respect to keep his burial place sacred.

HUGHES

That, too. So, I hope you'll forgive me, Mr. Power. I meant no disrespect. Nor did I mean to interrupt your story. Please go on now. You're doing a marvelous job!

POWER
As they passed the cemetery, the President had the carriage stop so that he and his wife could stroll through the peaceful surroundings. Then suddenly he grew serious and said to her: "Mary, when I am gone, lay my remains in some quiet place like this."

[Silence. They all stare at the sarcophagus in awe.]

MORRISEY
When it's a sarcophagus they lay you in, do they keep you in your casket?

POWER
Not in this case. The President arrived in an iron coffin which was stored in a receiving vault down the hill while the monument was built. When it came time to put him into the sarcophagus, however, the coffin would not fit. So, we had to move him to another coffin.

HUGHES
Move the corpse?

POWER
To a smaller coffin, one made of red cedar and lined with lead. Then we slid the new coffin into the sarcophagus, sealed it with the end plate, and closed the tomb door. At last, the President was laid to rest, six years after his death.

HUGHES
When you got a person what's been dead for so long, and then you have to open the casket for one reason or another, do you find yourself having a problem with the smell?

POWER
The President was embalmed on the morning after his assassination with a zinc chloride formula that forestalls much of the physical deterioration of death.

HUGHES
So, there would be no smell then?

POWER
The embalming process would reduce the smell, but not
eliminate it.

HUGHES
We're glad you're taking such good care of him.
This padlock, by the way. Is it how you protect him from
the public or have you other ways to secure the door as
well?

POWER
The padlock is what we use. It serves its purpose.

HUGHES
That reminds me. I happen to be a night watchman
looking for a job. Might you have a need here for a night
watchman?

POWER
No, I can't say that we do.

HUGHES
Well, you got me name and address in the visitor's book.
"James Smith from Racine." I hope you'll keep me in
mind if a position should open up.

POWER
Sir, I shall definitely keep you in mind.

HUGHES
How many guards do you employ here at night anyway?

POWER
[Pause. Fidgets.] We do not employ a night staff.

HUGHES
No night watchman?

POWER

The association has not seen the need for one. If there are no further questions—

MORRISSEY

[Points to numbered burial vaults in tomb.] Mr. Power, you never said what them numbers is for.

POWER

It's simply how we identify the vaults. The President's open crypt is Number One. In Number Two lie his sons William and Edward. In Number Three, his son Tad. The other two vaults are empty. They're reserved for the President's wife Mary and his son Robert.

HUGHES

So, it ain't just one corpse inside the tomb.

POWER

For now, it is a father and three sons.

HUGHES

I suppose even Presidents and their families go up the spout, eh? *[Silence. He is visibly shaken.]* Didn't know he had his boys with him.

[He and Morrissey look uneasily into the tomb.]

MORRISSEY

Well, we should be getting back downtown for the festivities. It's like a big circus with people yelling and drinking and making wagers on who'll be the next President!

POWER

I hear a fight broke out this morning near one of the polls. A man was murdered.

HUGHES

Election Day. It can be a dangerous time.

POWER

Thank you for your visit to the Lincoln Monument. Feel free to pay your last respects to the President before you depart.

[Power leaves. Hughes makes sure he is gone.]

HUGHES

One wee padlock, no guards, and a sarcophagus I could kick open like that. Oh, Jimmy Boy, if I was a religious man, I'd be down on me knees now thanking the Lord!

Scene IV

[The tomb entrance that night. The door is still padlocked shut. In the glow of a bull's-eye lantern and with a carpetbag beside him, Mullen is tediously sawing the staple that holds the lock. A whistle from outside. Morrissey and Hughes enter.]

HUGHES

So, you're still at it?

MULLEN

You can see I'm still at it. Billy Brown here yet?

MORRISSEY

Oh, yes. He's at the east gate now with a strong spring wagon and a rattling good pair of horses.

MULLEN

Hughes, how did the rig look to you?

HUGHES

Ain't seen the rig. Been checking the grounds to the west. Cold and dark, it is, with nobody about but the dead sleeping lonesome under their stones.

MULLEN

Ain't Billy Brown gonna help us break in?

MORRISSEY

No, he's got to stay at the gate and mind the horses. What's with that lock?

MULLEN

It's the most stubborn damned thing I ever come across in me bloody life. How long have I been sawing now anyway?

HUGHES

Long enough for anyone to wonder if you know what in hell you're doing.

MULLEN

Then you do it if you're so damned smart. Me arm is getting sore.

MORRISSEY

Maybe we should try the jimmy again.

HUGHES

[Takes over the sawing.] Nah, that jimmy's too big. You'll see, it's the saw what'll get us in. Just needs to be in the right hands, is all. When I was a lad in Cork, always wanted to grow up to be a—*[The saw suddenly breaks.]*—Jesus, Mary, and Joseph!

MORRISSEY

Are you all right, Jack?

HUGHES

Lemme see if I still got me fingers. One, two, three—

MULLEN

The blade snapped in half! So much for putting it in the right hands.

[Morrissey removes more tools from the carpetbag.]

MORRISSEY

We must have something for that staple. Axe. Hammer. Pinchers. Here we go, Boss. The three-cornered file. It's sharp enough.

MULLEN

Maybe so, but a little file like that on a piece of iron. It would take forever.

HUGHES

What about the powder and fuse we brung? I could mind the horses while Billy Brown blows this damned door to smithereens.

MORRISSEY

It's too still of a night for a noise like that. People would hear it and wonder what's up in that graveyard. We should use the file.

HUGHES

There's nobody around here but a bunch of dead people what ain't wondering nothing but who's that down there chewing at their toes.

MORRISSEY

What about the sexton?

HUGHES

Ain't nobody here at night. The old man said so.

MORRISSEY

He was talking about a guard for the monument, not a sexton for the graveyard. And, if there's a sexton, it's sure he lives nearby.

MULLEN

[Silence. Thinks about it.] Morrissey's right. We should use the file.

MORRISSEY
We'll take turns. Then it won't seem so bad.

HUGHES
You might as well go first, lad, being that you already got
it nicely situated in your hand.

MORRISSEY
All right, but I'm gonna need help. Come on, Jack. Reach
inside and around the bars. Then hold the lock steady
like this.

HUGHES
We should have brought a smaller jimmy.

*[Hughes holds the lock in place as Morrissey starts filing the
staple.]*

Scene V

MORRISSEY

Do you suppose we'll ever get in there?

MULLEN

All I know is, it's getting damned cold out. Pretty soon, it could be snowing.

HUGHES

Let's keep our minds on the two hundred thousand. That'll keep us warm.

MULLEN

That's something I been thinking about. The government might not want to part with their money unless they got somebody to arrest for the crime.

HUGHES

What in bleeding hell is this now? You want to get us arrested?

MULLEN

Not all of us. To look good in the eyes of the public, they'll need only one kidnapper.

HUGHES

And which kidnapper might that be?

MULLEN

Whoever volunteers. We will give this volunteer an extra ten thousand to spend a year in jail. I will also buy him a Brussels carpet for his cell so it'll look like a theatre, and bring him three meals a day so he won't have to eat no prison food. He'll live like a king!

HUGHES

So, I take it you ain't including yourself among them what might volunteer for jail.

MULLEN

I could hardly do that when I'm the public benefactor negotiating with the government.

HUGHES

I can't do it neither since I'm being exonerated from all charges of counterfeiting. To have them pardon me for one crime, then arrest me for another, it would make no sense.

MULLEN

Morrissey, would you like to be one amongst us what walks away with the most money?

MORRISSEY

Sure. Why not. Keep filing.

[Mullen and Hughes look at each other with surprise.]

Scene VI

[The tomb entrance later that night. Morrissey is now holding the lock in place as Mullen files. Hughes is looking at the sarcophagus.]

HUGHES
Poor Old Lincoln. They say he was a homely man.

MORRISSEY
You can see from his photographs he was a homely man.

HUGHES
They say he was even more homely in person than he was in his photographs. So homely his face was in person, they say, it made dogs howl and children cry.

MORRISSEY
Yet here he lies in this grand monument after emancipating the slaves and saving the Union. Goes to show, no matter who you are, you can do something important if you try.

MULLEN
There's many what says he was the worst President this country has known.

MORRISSEY

But everybody remembers him. What if you die and nobody ever thinks about you again?

HUGHES

What difference does it make when you're dead?

MORRISSEY

I don't know. I'm just tired after being up all night on the train looking out at Illinois in the dark. I never knew there was so much Illinois.

MULLEN

To hell with Illinois. Somebody grab them nippers.

HUGHES

Why? What's happening?

MULLEN

The nippers! Get 'em!

[Hughes does so. Wailing, Mullen uses the pinchers to twist and turn the lock. At last, the staple breaks. The lock falls off. The door creaks open.]

We're in!

[They enter in silence. They are all dumbstruck.]

HUGHES

Ain't this a sight now. Two coney men and a horse thief in the tomb of Abraham Lincoln!

MORRISSEY

Did you know, Mullen, that three of his children is in here, too? Buried in the wall behind them numbers.

MULLEN

Didn't know that.

MORRISSEY
Me, neither, but there they lie, toes up. Three boys what barely got to live their lives and a father what barely got to know his sons. No wonder Mrs. Lincoln went mad.

MULLEN
She went mad, did she?

MORRISSEY
Mad as a March hare. So, they locked her up and that's where she is on this very night. In a madhouse. After all the good that Abraham Lincoln done. You'd expect life to turn out better for him and his family.

HUGHES
Makes you wonder, if there's a God Upstairs, how could he let such things happen?

MULLEN
If there's anybody Upstairs, he long forgot about us down here. Now what are we doing anyway, having a church service or snatching a corpse?

MORRISSEY AND HUGHES
Snatching a corpse!

MULLEN
Then let's show some sand and get what we come for.

[Mullen grabs an axe and raises it to smash open the sarcophagus lid.]

MORRISSEY
No, wait, Boss, don't! You can't smash that apart!

MULLEN
You got any better ideas for getting it open?

MORRISSEY
Yeah, if you'd put down that ax and give me a moment to look on this.

MULLEN

You can look all you want. Any joker can see the lid is cemented on.

MORRISSEY

If we can get the lid off without damage, we can put it back in place when we're done and it won't be known the coffin is gone.

MULLEN

I know what I know and I am what I am. The only way to get that lid off is to smash it apart. And let me tell you, boys, I'm in the mood for some good smashing!

[He jams a crowbar under the sarcophagus lid.]

MORRISSEY

It crumbles apart. This ain't cement. It's Plaster of Paris!

HUGHES

What a world. After all the money they spent on this fancy tomb, they use bleeding Plaster of Paris to seal the old man in when no one's watching.

[Morrissey with the jimmy and Mullen with the axe start breaking the seal along the edges of the sarcophagus lid.]

MORRISSEY

This couldn't be more easy. Once the seal is broke, we can lift the lid right off.

MULLEN

It's as if they was begging us to take him.

[An echoing noise startles them. Another echoing noise. They all take out pistols. Hughes peers cautiously into the open burial vault.]

HUGHES

That sounded like it come from inside that bleeding

crypt. You lads believe in ghosts?

MULLEN

I don't believe in nothing I can't shoot. You two wait here while I look outside.

[With pistol drawn, Mullen leaves the tomb. Hughes peers into the open vault again. Another echoing noise.]

HUGHES

Maybe this weren't such a good idea after all.

MORRISSEY

What are you saying, Jack? That you want to leave?

HUGHES

It's all these dead people giving me the shakes. Especially Old Man Lincoln and them poor boys in the wall. Got a brother like that in Cork. Only it ain't a fancy crypt he's in. It's the cold hard earth. Been there since he was eleven, me dear brother Mike.

MORRISSEY

Was it the blight what done him in?

HUGHES

It was having a mother what couldn't afford a proper doctor. That's what me Mammy herself always says. Mike didn't die from the fever. He died from being poor.

MORRISSEY

You must miss him awful.

HUGHES

I do wonder what he would be like now. Meself as well. If I'd had me older brother Mike to guide me all these years, would I still be standing here in a bleeding tomb with a carpetbag full of tools?

MORRISSEY
Jack, why are you doing this?

HUGHES
I need the money.

MORRISSEY
Ever think about giving up the crooked life and finding
an honest job?

HUGHES
A man like me? Ain't nobody gonna hire Jack Hughes to
do nothing but shine his shoes.

MORRISSEY
At least you'd be working for the good of society.

HUGHES
So?

MORRISSEY
So ain't that what they say you're supposed to be doing?

HUGHES
They say all sorts of things. Most of it don't add up to a
hill of beans when you're hungry. Besides, d'you really
think we're that different from the buggers what run the
banks? We're all doing the same thing, only we're doing
it with more style!

MORRISSEY
When I'm an old man looking back on me life, I don't
want to regret what I done.

HUGHES
You think you're gonna regret this?

MORRISSEY
I don't know, Jack. It's complicated. Is this truly what you
want to be doing? Robbing a good man's grave?

HUGHES

It ain't that I "want" to be doing it, but—

MORRISSEY

It ain't too late to change your mind. You could leave right now.

HUGHES

After all our trouble to get this far, tell me how in hell I could do that.

MORRISSEY

It's simple. You walk out the door.

[Silence. They both look at the door.]

HUGHES

Suppose I did walk out. Would you be walking with me, Jimmy?

MORRISSEY

I ain't sure, Jack. Didn't know we'd be having this conversation.

HUGHES

Me neither, but here we are having it. Now why do you suppose that is?

MORRISSEY

Anything can happen, I guess, when you got Abraham Lincoln in the room.

[They stare in awe at the sarcophagus. Long silence.]

What are you thinking about?

HUGHES

The two hundred thousand. That's one hell of a lot of rhino.

MORRISSEY
Not if something goes wrong. Something goes wrong, ain't no rhino at all.

HUGHES
Wait a minute, Jimmy. You know something I don't?

[A whistle from outside. Morrissey returns.]

MULLEN
The coast is clear. Somebody gimme that axe so I can get this damned thing open. *[No one moves. Silence.]* I said, gimme the axe somebody. Is there a problem?

HUGHES
What if we go to all of this trouble and then we don't get the money?

MULLEN
We got it all planned out. Why wouldn't we get the money?

HUGHES
I don't know. Ask him.

MULLEN
What the hell did you say to him while I was outside?

MORRISSEY
Nothing, Boss. We got the shakes, is all, from hearing them noises.

MULLEN
You think we ain't gonna get the money?

MORRISSEY
No, sir, I never said that. I—

MULLEN
[Shoves Morrissey.] You're getting me Irish up. Don't do that, Morrissey. Don't get me Irish up.

HUGHES

Leave the lad alone, for crying out loud. He ain't done nothing wrong.

MULLEN

He ain't answered me question. *[Shoves Morrissey again.]* Why do you think we ain't getting the money?

MORRISSEY

I only said that "if" something goes wrong—

MULLEN

Look, I come here for a reason and I ain't stopping now. So, if you jokers ain't with me, I'll get Billy Brown to help. Then me and him, we'll be rich men counting our money while you Miss Nancy's are at the poor house shaking in the corner.

MORRISSEY

We never said we wasn't with you, Boss.

HUGHES

And I ain't no Miss Nancy!

MULLEN

Then somebody gimme the bloody axe so we can get this damned lid off!

[Morrissey does so and gets the jimmy for himself. They continue to break the sarcophagus seal.]

HUGHES

I'll tell you lads something and I don't mind admitting it neither. This is the first time in me life I can finally say I'm doing something big. Ever since I was a boy, I been cursed with a small view of the world. Like back in Philadelphia when I was still making the coney meself. What did I make? Ten dollar bills? Five dollar bills? No, what Jack Hughes made was nickels. That's me.

The Nickel Man. But look at me now, lads. I couldn't get no further from them nickels if I tried!

MORRISSEY

If it makes you that happy, Jack, maybe you're in the right place after all.

MULLEN

Okay, the seal is broke. Every man find his side so we can twist the lid and lift her off.

[They surround the sarcophagus. Each grips the lid.]

This is it, boys. Go slow and think strong.

[They twist the lid crosswise, lift it up, and carry it to the wall where they lean it upright. They return to the sarcophagus. Morrissey starts to gag. Hughes covers his nose with a handkerchief.]

HUGHES

Smells like a bleeding pig farm!

MORRISSEY

That ain't no pig farm. It's Mr. Death himself rising up to greet us.

MULLEN

It's only a little stink. Let's see what we got.

[Mullen holds the lantern over the sarcophagus to inspect the exposed lid of Lincoln's coffin.]

MORRISSEY

His wooden coat!

MULLEN

How do we lift it out? It's so damned snug, there's nothing to grab hold of.

HUGHES

We'll have to open it up and remove him.

MULLEN
The lid is screwed on and we ain't got no screwdriver.
Let's smash it open.

MORRISSEY
Smash the coffin?

MULLEN
We got to do something. If we can't lift the coffin out—

MORRISSEY
No, you can't smash the coffin! Why do you want to
smash everything?

MULLEN
What do we bloody care? We're grave robbers.

MORRISSEY
Then at least be practical. They ain't gonna pay two
hundred thousand for a body what's been chopped at.

HUGHES
As usual, he's got a good point.

MULLEN
We ain't got no other choice. But don't worry. I'll be
careful.

MORRISSEY
You can't be careful when you're swinging an axe. And
how would we carry the body if we don't got no coffin?

MULLEN
With the sack I brung. We'll slide him into that, then
carry him out like a big potato.

MORRISSEY
Hold on. When we was here today, the old man said they
"slid" the coffin into the sarcophagus. What slides in,
slides out. I bet that head plate comes off.

HUGHES

He's right. Look. It's only some copper ties holding it in place.

MULLEN

Them bloody ties is asking for it, mates. Let's show 'em who's boss.

[With tools from the carpetbag, Mullen and Hughes start to break the ties atop each corner of the end plate.]

MORRISSEY

While you fellas do that, I'm gonna step outside to have a cigar.

MULLEN

A cigar? Hughes, you ever seen Morrissey smoke a cigar?

HUGHES

No, I ain't never seen him smoke a cigar.

MULLEN

Seems like a peculiar time to be starting up a new vice.

MORRISSEY

Been smoking all me life. See? Got a cigar right here and I'll be back in a jiffy.

MULLEN

[Aims pistol at Morrissey.] Hold it, paddy! You ain't going nowhere!

HUGHES

What in hell are you doing? That's our partner you're gonna shoot!

MULLEN

Check outside. See if anybody's waiting there.

HUGHES

This is a graveyard in the middle of the night. Who would be waiting there?

MULLEN

Just look, damn it, and give the whistle before you come back in.

[Hughes goes outside. Mullen disarms Morrissey.]

Keep your hands where I can see 'em.

MORRISSEY

Boss, why are you turning on me like this?

MULLEN

I'm just always cautious around people from Wicklow.

MORRISSEY

This ain't no time to be going against a pal. Not when we're finally gonna get what we want. Look at it, Boss. It's right there. How many people ever get this close to what they want? All we have to do is reach out and take it.

MULLEN

Oh, I ain't going nowhere without my President. I just hope you ain't got no other vices we ain't aware of.

[A whistle from outside. Hughes returns.]

HUGHES

Everybody out there is still dead.

MULLEN

Let's hope it stays that way.

HUGHES

I don't know what's going through that bleeding head of yours, but we got work to do. So, put the gun away and help me with this damned head plate.

MULLEN

[Puts pistol away.] I'm watching you, Morrissey. And me eyes still ain't sure they're liking what they see.

MORRISSEY

What about me pistol?

MULLEN

I'll be minding it for you 'til our work here is done.

HUGHES

Oh, for crying out loud, give the poor lad his pistol.

MULLEN

I ain't giving him no pistol!

MORRISSEY

He can keep the pistol for now, but I need some fresh air. The smell is making me ill.

MULLEN

We ain't got time for that. Grab the lantern and hold it here so we can see what we're doing!

[Morrissey doesn't move. He looks at door.]

Let's go, paddy! The lantern! We ain't got all bloody night!

[Morrissey gets the lantern. He holds it for them as they continue to detach the head plate.]

HUGHES

How do we know Old Lincoln is really in here?

MULLEN

He's dead and this is his bloody coffin. Where else would he be?

HUGHES

Right now, I'd believe anything.

MULLEN
Maybe you're right. Once we get the coffin out, we'll pry it open and have a peek inside.

MORRISSEY
No, the coffin must not be damaged!

HUGHES
Jimmy, I hate to say this, but it is a wee bit odd you're acting tonight.

MORRISSEY
I just don't want no damage to the coffin. Nor do I wish to see the face inside.

MULLEN
We thought you was "the boss body snatcher of Chicago."

MORRISSEY
Aye, and it's known rule in the trade you never look at the face of anyone you resurrect. That's a face what would haunt you forever.

MULLEN
I ain't afraid of looking at his face. If he still got one.

HUGHES
What if Jimmy is right? What if we see the face of Abraham Lincoln and then we're haunted for the rest of our lives?

MULLEN
What's with you two? You act like you're ready to join Mrs. Lincoln in that madhouse.

HUGHES
We're just being respectful of the dead is what we're being.

[Hughes tosses the head plate aside with a loud thud.]

MULLEN

All right, let's get that bloody casket out! You, too, Morrissey! Give us a hand!

[They surround the coffin and struggle to move it out of the sarcophagus. The coffin doesn't budge.]

HUGHES

This must be the heaviest damned thing I ever tried to move in me life.

MORRISSEY

It's the lead lining what makes it heavy.

MULLEN

No, mate, what makes it heavy is your future. That's what's in there. Everything you ever wanted from the day you was born. Now show some muscle, you miserable sons of Erin!

[They resume the struggle. The coffin starts to move.]

Jesus Christ, boys, we're doing it!

[The coffin slowly slides out − fifteen inches. They stop, exhausted, and look at the coffin in silence.]

HUGHES

There's no way in hell we're ever gonna pick that up, let alone carry it.

MULLEN

You can't give up now. It's half way out.

HUGHES

The Devil is me uncle if that's half way out.

[They look at one other helplessly. Mullen suddenly breaks down and begins to sob.]

Mullen, are you all right? Terrance?

MULLEN
  WHY MUST EVERYTHING ALWAYS BE SO
  BLOODY DIFFICULT?

[Silence. Mullen begins sobbing again.]

MORRISSEY
  Look, we can do this, but we need our fourth man.
  Wait here while I get Billy Brown.

HUGHES
  Good idea, lad, and hurry! We need to finish this before
  we all go loony.

MULLEN
  Tell him to remember the whistle.

HUGHES
  Don't forget to whistle before you come back in.
  Otherwise we might fire at you, thinking you're someone
  else.

MULLEN
  We ain't gonna let no one come monkeying around
  here!

*[Morrissey starts to leave, but stops at the tomb door.
He looks at Hughes for a moment.]*

MORRISSEY
  Jack, I'm sorry.

HUGHES
  What's that, lad?

MORRISSEY
  I'm sorry about your brother Mike.

[Hughes looks at him curiously. Morrissey leaves.]

HUGHES
That Morrissey, he really is kind of an odd duck.

[An echoing noise startles them. Another echoing noise. Mullen starts putting tools back into the carpetbag.]

MULLEN
That's enough of this bloody tomb. Let's pack up and wait for the boys outside.

HUGHES
Down the hill by the dark of the trees we can sit. That way we'll see when they're coming.

MULLEN
Don't you worry, Mr. President. Soon as we got our fourth man, we'll be back to—

[A GUNSHOT from afar. They look at each other in horror and draw their pistols. They look around and then flee with the carpetbag, leaving behind the lantern and a few tools. Silence.]

TYRRELL'S VOICE
[From a distance.] THIS IS THE UNITED STATES SECRET SERVICE! YOU ARE SURROUNDED! LAY DOWN YOUR ARMS AND SURRENDER WITH YOUR HANDS RAISED!

[With revolver drawn, Tyrrell appears outside the tomb in his stocking feet. He has a white handkerchief around his arm.]

TYRRELL
GRAVE ROBBERS! WE KNOW YOU ARE IN THERE! COME OUT NOW AND SURRENDER PEACEFULLY!

[He cautiously enters the tomb and sees that Mullen and Hughes are gone. He takes a quick look around.]

Damnation!

[Morrissey runs in. He is now wearing a white arm band as well.]

MORRISSEY

Sir, they ain't here no more! McGinn says—

TYRRELL

Who the hell fired that shot? McGinn?

MORRISSEY

No, sir, it was Hay, but McGinn says—

TYRRELL

He let the bastards know we were here! What in God's name was he shooting at?

MORRISSEY

It was an accident, sir. He didn't mean to fire.

TYRRELL

And he calls himself a Pinkerton? Where the hell are the Pinkertons?

MORRISSEY

Searching the grounds, sir. McGinn seen the boys out by the trees!

TYRRELL

Let's go! Maybe it's not too late!

MORRISSEY

Wait! Mullen took me pistol! I got no weapon!

TYRRELL

Stay here then, and be careful! Someone could get killed!

[Tyrrell races out. After a moment, there is a loud GUNSHOT outside. Morrissey takes cover behind the sarcophagus.

A GUNSHOT is returned from afar.

Another loud GUNSHOT outside.

Two more GUNSHOTS from afar.

Distant COMMOTION begins.]

TYRRELL'S VOICE
THE DEVILS ARE UP HERE! SURROUND THE MONUMENT! GET UP HERE, MEN, AND CATCH THESE DEVILS! CHIEF, WE HAVE THE DEVILS UP HERE!

MAN'S VOICE
[From afar.] TYRRELL, IS THAT YOU? *[No reply.]* TYRRELL, FOR GOD'S SAKE, ANSWER! IS THAT YOU?

Scene VII

[Later that night. Swegles huddles beside the coffin as Tyrrell stands at the door. They are both in deep shock.]

TYRRELL
In all my life, this is one of the most unfortunate nights I have ever experienced.

[Silence.]

Lewis, are you all right? *[No reply.]* Morrissey? *[No reply.]* Tell me at least who you are now so I know what to call you.

SWEGLES
Swegles. Lewis Swegles.

TYRRELL
So, you're all right.

SWEGLES
Yes, sir. And the others?

TYRRELL
Chief Washburn has sprained his ankle. Everyone else seems to be all right.

SWEGLES
Hughes and Mullen?

TYRRELL
They've escaped. We're combing the area for evidence.

SWEGLES
So, they didn't get shot neither.

TYRRELL
No one got shot.

SWEGLES
Why so much gunfire? I worried that…

TYRRELL
Someone ran up to the terrace. I didn't see his white arm band in the dark. Only a figure behind a column. I aimed and fired. As it turns out, I was – God help us all – I was shooting at Detective McGinn. And Detective McGinn was shooting back at me.

[He inspects the premises. Looks at the lantern and tools that were left behind.]

The fiends may be gone, but the marks of their Devilish work are plainly visible.

SWEGLES
This ain't nothing compared to what might have been.

TYRRELL
We should consider ourselves blessed. God protected us in doing right and granted us an escape from death most miraculous. For that, I thank God from the bottom of my heart. However, this does not make for a good report to Washington. Why did you wait so long to give us the password?

SWEGLES
Huh?

TYRRELL

You were to let us know the instant the sarcophagus was open. We would then traverse the one hundred and twenty paces from the front of the monument to the—

SWEGLES

Sir, I do know what the plan was and I did my best to follow it.

TYRRELL

Did you?

SWEGLES

Yes, sir, why would you think otherwise?

TYRRELL

You have expressed sympathy for these men.

SWEGLES

Is that what you're going to write in your report?

TYRRELL

My report will include all that occurred here tonight. Washington will have many questions, as will the Lincoln Monument Association.

SWEGLES

Mr. Lincoln has been protected. That's what you need to tell them.

TYRRELL

I assured Robert Lincoln and Mr. Power both that the grave robbers would be caught. I also gave my solemn word that the coffin would not be touched. Look at this coffin!

SWEGLES

It's only pulled out a small way.

TYRRELL

This is the coffin of President Abraham Lincoln! Now the hands of ghouls have been laid upon it! And look here, the lid is chipped! Did you see this chip? This should not be!

SWEGLES

If Mullen'd had his way, you would be looking now at a sarcophagus smashed into pieces and an empty coffin hacked open with an axe!

TYRRELL

But if you had given the password sooner, the coffin would still be in the sarcophagus and the grave robbers might now be under arrest!

SWEGLES

It ain't my fault a Pinkerton's gun went off and scared them away!

TYRRELL

Was it the gunshot that led to their escape or the extra time they had to smell trouble?

SWEGLES

It was the gunshot! You said so yourself!

TYRRELL

We have no way to know what would have occurred if you had followed the plan.

SWEGLES

Are you going to blame me for Mullen and Hughes getting away?

TYRRELL

In the end, I shall blame myself since I am the one in charge. After this night, I had hoped to be greeted by the Department as a hero, but instead I shall be seen as a fool who runs through cemeteries in his stocking feet and shoots at Pinkertons.

SWEGLES
You still ain't said how I fit into that.

TYRRELL
The practice of using ropers is a controversial one. Many in the Department believe that criminals do not make good agents. When things go wrong and a roper is involved, it stokes the fires of their criticism.

SWEGLES
I know I ain't no middle-class man. Don't own a house in a respectable part of town. Nor sit in a fancy office and write reports. But look at me. Am I really so different from you? Or Mr. Power? Or the Pinkertons? Or the fucking Department?

TYRRELL
Watch yourself, Lewis. You've been under a lot of strain and you don't know what you're saying.

SWEGLES
I know exactly what I'm saying. I want credit for what I done!

TYRRELL
Credit for what? A desecrated tomb and a damaged coffin?

SWEGLES
You said I would be a hero, get my name in the newspaper!

TYRRELL
If you had been successful, yes, you would have been the man who put Mullen and Hughes behind bars.

SWEGLES
I don't want to be the man who put Mullen and Hughes

behind bars. I want to be the man who protected Abraham Lincoln!

TYRRELL

It's one and the same thing.

SWEGLES

No, your purpose was to arrest men you think of as filthy swine. My purpose was to protect Abraham Lincoln. That's what I set out to do. That's what I done. And it ain't my damned fault that the lid of the coffin is chipped!

TYRRELL

[Pause. Bristles.] We will continue this in my office on Thursday after you've had a good night's rest and time to think about what you're saying. If you hurry, you can still catch the midnight train to Chicago. Here is your payment for today.

[He holds up five dollars. Swegles doesn't take it.]

Take your payment. You've worked hard for the money.

SWEGLES

You think I do this only for the money?

TYRRELL

I don't care why you do it. I only care that you do it well. Now take what's yours and go.

SWEGLES

If you're writing reports, sir, you need to know something, sir, that you don't seem to know. This ain't easy! Trying to be what I ain't! Doing things vile and loathsome! Telling lies 'til I don't know what's what or who's who! Am I Swegles pretending to be Morrissey or Morrissey pretending to be Swegles? I been through a lot here, a hell of a lot, and it ain't for the five dollars you put in my hand at the end of the day!

TYRRELL

I'm glad to know you have a noble purpose. We will discuss it on Thursday.

SWEGLES

It won't matter on Thursday. After all I done, you'll still be looking at me the same way. It's the way you looked at me when I first come to your office and the way you're looking at me now.

TYRRELL

And how is it that you think I look at you?

SWEGLES

Like I ain't nothing but a damned horse thief.

[Silence. Swegles snatches the money from Tyrrell.

They stare at each other for a moment.

Swegles throws the money to the floor and walks out.]

Scene VIII

[Twenty years later. Older Nealy with a newspaper, as we saw him in Scene 1. While he speaks, spotlights rise and fall on the other men when he refers to them. Each stands alone, as if awaiting judgment.]

OLDER NEALY

November seventh, 1876. It was a moonless night when nobody got what they wanted. Not even the American people, for the election that night could not be settled, and it would be another four months before the White House could finally be claimed by Rutherford B. Hayes.

[Spotlights on Mullen and Hughes each facing us.]

Terrance Mullen and Jack Hughes left Oak Ridge without the treasure they had sought and returned to Chicago as if nothing had occurred. A few nights later, they was arrested at The Hub by—

[Spotlight on Tyrrell. Facing us.]

—Captain Patrick D. Tyrrell. Grave robbing was not yet a felony, so he charged them with the worst he could: conspiracy to steal a coffin worth seventy-five dollars.

Both was convicted and served one year in the Illinois State Penitentiary.

[Mullen and Hughes vanish. Spotlight on Nelson facing us.]

Herbert Nelson was also arrested but, due to lack of evidence, all charges against him was dropped. The same was true of Big Jim Kennally, the invisible man they called "Cornelius," even though it was him who had thought the whole thing up.

[Nelson and Tyrrell vanish. Spotlight on Swegles facing us.]

As for Lewis Swegles, he finally got his name in the newspaper for something other than stealing horses. Some hailed him as a hero for what he done. But others wasn't so sure. At the trial of Mullen and Hughes, most of the jury thought that it was Lewis who'd been the true mastermind of the plot and that he'd tried to use everyone else, including the Secret Service, to make himself rich. After that, Lewis disappeared like a cat in the night.

[Swegles vanishes.]

Nothing more did I hear from Lewis nor about him 'til a few years later when he made the news again. This time he had been arrested for burglary and sentenced to twelve years in the Joliet State Prison.

Now all them twelve long years has passed by plus a few years more. And here he is in the newspaper again. Found his name this morning in the back section.

"Lewis Cass Swegles."

A friend of mine, he was, and a man of many talents. Sailor, horse thief, burglar, roper, who knows what else. He weren't a roper for long, but that's how I like to think of him. As the Prince of Ropers. For what might have happened to President Abraham Lincoln if it hadn't been for Lewis Swegles?

Thank you for your service to your country, Mr. Swegles.

Rest in peace, sir.

You are not forgotten.

[A moment of silence.]

END OF PLAY

CAMPFIRE

Joseph Zettelmaier

A horror play. Marcus Carver has brought his niece and nephew back home. In the woods behind his farm, around a campfire, the Carvers will tell stories as they have for many generations. But a stranger has entered the dimly-lit circle.

Captain Blood

David Rice

Unjustly sentenced to slavery on a Caribbean island, the bold Dr. Peter Blood falls in love with the lady of the plantation, the lovely Arabella Bishop. When Blood escapes and takes up the life of a pirate, it appears that fate has separated them forever...or has it? Filled with sword fights and pirate battles, love and treachery, and even a song or two, *Captain Blood* is a pirate adventure perfect for the whole crew!

Churchill

Ronald Keaton

March 1946. After leading Britain and her Allies to victory in the European Theatre, Winston Churchill has been shockingly defeated for re-election as Prime Minister. Living in forced retirement, Churchill receives an invitation from President Harry Truman to speak at Westminster College in Fulton, Missouri, where he will deliver his legendary, emphatic "Iron Curtain" speech.

The Count of Monte Cristo

Christopher M. Walsh

Framed by a conspiracy and torn from the woman he loves, Edmond Dantes is wrongly imprisoned for fourteen years. Escaping captivity, he enters the upper reaches of Parisian society, insinuating himself into the lives of his three tormentors as, one by one, he seeks to use their own secrets to destroy them in the guise of his new identity: the Count of Monte Cristo. A dark tale of intrigue and vengeance by epic storyteller Alexandre Dumas.

THE DECADE DANCE

JOSEPH ZETTELMAIER

A one-night stand becomes a ten-year journey as Rog and Nina navigate a relationship against the backdrop of a turbulent decade. A touching two-hander, carefully balancing nostalgia, romance, and humor as two people live unexpected lives.

DEAD MAN'S SHOES

JOSEPH ZETTELMAIER

A dark and hilarious western, with a dash of buddy-comedy. Notorious outlaw Injun Bill Picote has escaped from prison, along with a hard-luck drunk named Froggy. The unlikely partners endure trials and bizarre misadventures as they set out to right a terrible wrong.

DR. SEWARD'S DRACULA

JOSEPH ZETTELMAIER

Dr. Seward has cut himself off from the rest of the world after losing his lover and friends to Dracula. The Irish author Bram Stoker wishes to tell his story. Soon, a series of murders occur, very similar to the ones Seward fought to stop. A re-imagining of Bram Stoker's Dracula.

EBENEZER: A CHRISTMAS PLAY

JOSEPH ZETTELMAIER

It's a cold Christmas Eve in London, and Ebenezer Scrooge sits in a hospital room. 15 years have passed since his miraculous transformation by the Ghosts of Christmas. They are about to return for a final judgment. Based on Charles Dickens' classic *A Christmas Carol*.

EVE OF IDES
DAVID BLIXT

The night before his assassination at the hands of conspirators, Julius Caesar attended a feast. With him were Brutus, Cassius, and Antony. During the meal, Caesar was asked what he thought was the best way to die. Caesar answered, 'What does it matter, so long as it's quick?' Based on history and the works of Shakespeare, *Eve Of Ides* reveals the unexplored relationship between the main players of the age — Caesar, Brutus, and Antony.

FRANKENSTEIN
ROBERT KAUZLARIC

When an unexpected death shatters her family, Victoria retreats into the darkest recesses of her psyche in search of a way forward. To find meaning in this impossible loss, she brings a terrible creation to life — one whose existence threatens all hopes for the future. Haunted and hunted at every turn, Victoria must endure a nightmare journey of the soul in a quest for survival. A brilliant reimagining of the 1818 thriller by Mary Wollstonecraft Shelley.

THE GRAVEDIGGER
JOSEPH ZETTELMAIER

A gothic drama inspired by Mary Shelly's classic novel. In one of Bavaria's forgotten cemeteries, a lone gravedigger discovers a hideously scarred man hiding in a fresh grave. What the gravedigger doesn't know is that the man is none other than the legendary monster created by a mad doctor. What the scarred man doesn't know is the gravedigger's hand in his creation. And what neither men know is that they are hunted by their shared past.

HATFIELD & MCCOY
SHAWN PFAUTSCH

When a forbidden love affair ignites the simmering tensions between two families, the stage is set for an explosive clash that threatens to consume them all. Secrets unravel, alliances shift, and long-buried grudges resurface as the Hatfields and McCoys hurtle towards an inevitable and deadly confrontation.

HER MAJESTY'S WILL
ROBERT KAUZLARIC

Young William Shakespeare is hiding from the law in rural Lancashire, languishing as a simple school master. Christopher Marlowe is living the high life as a spy for the Crown. When a dastardly plot to assassinate the Queen draws these two unforgettable wits together, Will is swept up in a world of intrigue, treachery, and mayhem in an adventure that will define the rest of his life — if he can only manage to survive it. Based on the novel by David Blixt.

THE HOUSE OF IDEAS
MARK PRACHT

Its the 1960s, and Marvel Comics is redefining pop culture. Behind the scenes, two visionaries, writer Stan Lee and artist Jack Kirby, built a shared universe that changed comics forever. But as Marvel's fortunes climb, so do tensions between its architects. Who truly deserves credit for The House of Ideas?

THE INNOCENCE OF SEDUCTION
MARK PRACHT

The Innocence of Seduction examines the 1950s Congressional investigation into the supposed link between comic books and juvenile delinquency, and the effect of the investigation on the careers of three persons: William Gaines, the originator of the horror genre of comic books; Matt Baker, a Black closeted gay artist of romance comics; and Janice Valleau, creator of a pioneering comics feature starring a woman detective.

IT CAME FROM MARS
JOSEPH ZETTELMAIER

A hilarious look at the night of Orson Welles' famous *War Of The Worlds* broadcast! The members of Farlowe's Mystery Theatre Hour are in rehearsal for their weekly radio show when they hear an alarming announcement come over the radio—Martians have landed! Suddenly secrets are revealed as the cast and crew believe it is their last night on earth!

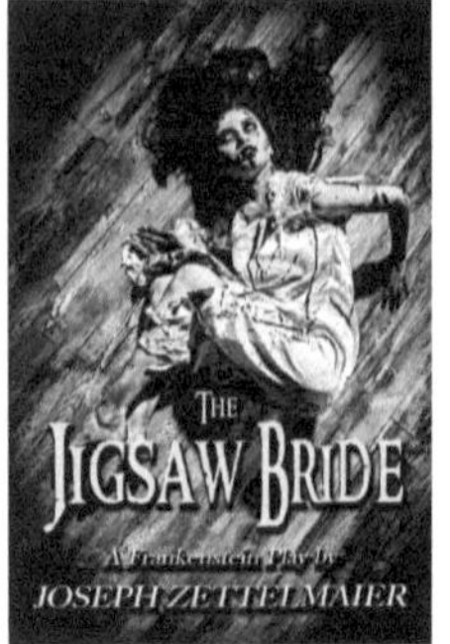

THE JIGSAW BRIDE
JOSEPH ZETTELMAIER

A century after Victor Frankenstein's demise, the brilliant scientist Maria von Moos unearths his secrets when she stumbles upon a mesmerizing discovery — Justine, a woman frozen in time. Maria brings Justine into her home, setting the stage for a captivating odyssey of science and hope.

THE LEAGUE OF AWESOME
CORRBETTE PASKO & SARA SEVIGNY

The superheroes of The League Of Awesome have done it again. They decided to punish the SorrowMaker by trapping him inside a Hardy Boys book. Yeah, it was a little unconventional. Zoe, Sylvia, Penny, Kitty & Rumble wouldn't let him escape. I mean....come on! They'd have to be drunk to do that! Now let's watch them celebrate their victory over him with mojitos. Oh...oh dear.

MALAPERT LOVE
SIAH BERLATSKY

A hilarious mash-up/homage/reimagining of classical comedic elements! *Malapert Love* is a modern response to the tropes, style and structure of Shakespeare's comedies. It follows the tangled and farcical action of a group of people who have all fallen in love with the wrong person.

THE MAN-BEAST
JOSEPH ZETTELMAIER

The wilds of France are stalked by a fearsome creature—the Beast of Gévaudan. An outcast forester presents its corpse to King Louis for a rich reward. However, the story he told may not have been the entire truth. Based on the legends of the loupe-garou, the famous French warewolf.

THE MAN WHO WAS THURSDAY
BILAL DARDAI

When Gabriel Syme joins the undercover detail tasked with infiltrating an anarchists' operations, he soon finds himself sitting on their Supreme Council with the code name "Thursday." It slowly becomes clear that no one in this battle between law and chaos is as they seem — and that Scotland Yard may have created the very problem they're trying to solve. Uncover the truth in this absorbing adaptation of the 1908 satire by G. K. Chesterton.

THE MARK OF KANE
MARK PRACHT

In 1939, two young friends huddled in a Bronx apartment and created a legend, a caped crusader who represents an enduring chapter in the tale of the American comic book. One, Bob Kane, would profit from that legend for years to come. The other, Bill Finger, would be all but forgotten. This is the legacy of the mark of Kane.

THE MOONSTONE
ROBERT KAUZLARIC

The Moonstone, an Indian diamond steeped in a history of violence and mysticism, is stolen from Rachel Verinder's sitting room, and no one in her household is above suspicion. Join an unforgettable collection of liars, lovers, addicts and outcasts as they struggle to uncover the truth and reclaim the stone before its curse destroys them all. This thrilling mystery by Wilkie Collins is regarded as the first detective novel in the English language.

MY ITALY STORY/LONG GONE DADDY
JOSEPH GALLO

Spurred by visits from his grandmother's ghost, Thomas DaGato quits his job as a New York account executive, and travels to the tiny Italian village of his ancestors—Vallata. The sequel play chronicles the comic misadventures of becoming a stay-at-home father.

ONCE A PONZI TIME

JOE FOUST

For years, Harold has 'helped' his friends with their investments, but his artful dodging and shady shenanigans are about to collapse around him as his pyramid scheme tumbles to earth. With only the help of his flakey father, his naive nephew, and a ventriloquist's dummy, can Harold hoodwink the Russian mob, bamboozle the SEC, and restore his friends' fortunes without his entire world becoming a complete farce? Watch him try!

THE SCULLERY MAID

JOSEPH ZETTELMAIER

Having declared an uneasy truce in England's ongoing war with France, King Edward III and his nobles celebrate in Nottingham Castle. Unbeknownst to the king, a murder plot is being hatched in the kitchen by the lowliest of his servants, who seeks revenge to right the wrongs of a lifetime. Religion, politics, and questions of loyalty, all at a knife's edge.

ANTON CHEKHOV'S THE SEAGULL

JANICE L. BLIXT & ALEXANDRA LACOMBE

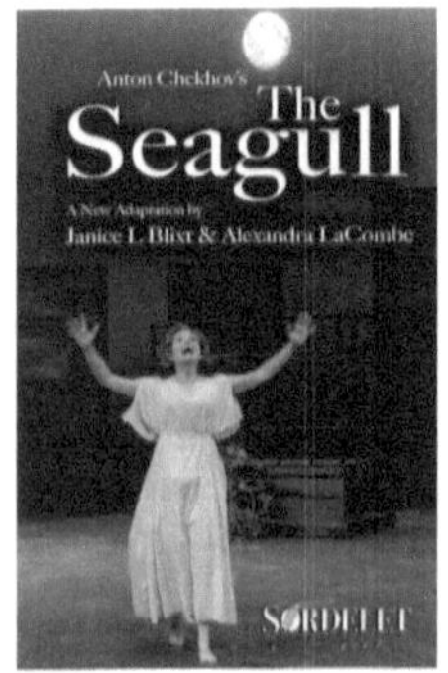

This new translation of Anton Chekhov's classic *The Seagull* restores what most English-language versions of the play omit: humor. Considered a world-class humorist and wit, Chekov intended this play to be a Comedy. Translated by Alexandra LaCombe and adapted by award-winning director Janice L. Blixt, this is *The Seagull* audiences have been waiting for.

SEASON ON THE LINE

SHAWN PFAUTSCH

A novice assistant stage manager joins the crew of Bad Settlement Theatre Company for their make-or-break season. An aging artistic director is hell-bent on mounting the elusive perfect staging of *Moby Dick*. The play swings from soliloquy to action-adventure story as the young man grows to love the theatrical live, even a those around him pay the ultimate price for their pursuit of theatre's own great white whale.

SHOCK! THE SPINE-TINGLING TALE OF MISS SPIDRA

JOSEPH ZETTELMAIER

Her fans never knew Joyce Billings. To them, she was Miss Spidra, campy host of The Night Parlor, Toledo's midnight horror movie show. Starting as a struggling actress trying to make her mark, Joyce finds herself becoming an icon, a celebrity. But her efforts to keep her beloved show alive cost her more than she could have guessed.

A TALE OF TWO CITIES

CHRISTOPHER M. WALSH

The Reign of Terror sweeps through Paris, and two Londoners are confronted with impossible choices. Will aristocratic Charles Darnay abandon his family to protect an innocent man? Can depressive barrister Sydney Carton make the ultimate sacrifice for unrequited love? An epic story of resurrection and redemption, based on the 1859 novel by Charles Dickens.

VOICES IN THE DARK

JOSEPH ZETTELMAIER

Turn out the lights and shiver with delight at this anthology collection of seven short horror radio plays by renowned horror writer Joseph Zettelmaier.

THE WHITE ROAD

KAREN TARJAN

The story of Ernest Shackleton's ill-fated attempt to cross Antarctica from sea to sea via the South Pole. The crew is forced to abandon their ship, The Endurance, having been crushed by pack ice. They have one path ahead: The White Road. Experience an incredible story of survival, under near impossible conditions, and a display of the strength of the human spirit when all hope appears lost.

OTHER WORKS FROM
SORDELET INK
WWW.SORDELETINK.COM

HOLD, PLEASE
STAGE MANAGING A PANDEMIC

RICHARD HESTER

A pandemic chronicle from the particular point of view of a career Broadway stage manager living in Manhattan. Part journal, part blog, these essays attempted to make sense of the crisis and what it was doing to us. By the end, everything had changed. What follows is a journey through one of the most fascinating periods in both our cultural and our personal histories.

NELLIE BLY'S WORLD
VOL. 1 — 3

BY NELLIE BLY

Bly's complete reporting, collected for the very first time! Starting with the stunt that made hers a household name, Nellie Bly spends her first year at the New York World going undercover to expose frauds, sharpsters and boodlers, interviewing Belva Lockwood and Hangman Joe, and tackling Phelps the Lobbyist!

INTO THE MADHOUSE
BY NELLIE BLY

Never before collected! "Who is this insane girl?" asked other papers, completely taken in by Nellie Bly's plan to infiltrate Blackwell's Island. The complete reporting surrounding her daring expose, including details not included in her initial accounts and her scathing rebuttal of the doctors' excuses!

Books by Nellie Bly

the Lost Novels

the Mystery of Central Park
Eva the Adventuress
New York by Night
Alta Lynn, m.d.
Wayne's Faithful Sweetheart
Little Luckie
In Love With a Stranger
the Love of Three Girls
Little Penny, Child of the Streets
Pretty Merribelle
Twins & Rivals

Reporting

Into the Madhouse
Nellie Bly's World Vol 1-4
Nellie Bly's Dispatches Vol 1-2
Nellie Bly's Journal Vol 1-2

VISIT WWW.SORDELETINK.COM